E

"I need to be a p____
life," Sam said w____
"This baby need____

Joy shivered with cold apprehension. "This is
ridiculous."

"No, it's not." He put a hand on her shoulder
when she turned away. He forced her to face
him. Leaning down, he stared into her eyes. His
determined gaze looked like solid steel and made
her knees weak. "There's a simple solution."

"What?" She lifted her chin defiantly.

"We have to get married," he said, his voice
low and husky, warm and gentle, firm and
uncompromising. His hand touched her stomach
again, connecting them once more in a common
bond.

The familiarity and intimacy of the gesture
combined was an assault on Joy's senses. Her
mind reeled. Her ears filled with the sound of
pumping blood. "What?"

His gaze softened, and he touched the corner of
her mouth with his thumb. "Marry me."

* * *

"*Open in Nine Months* is a touching, emotional
story, a perfect way to put yourself into the
holiday spirit."

—Judy Christenberry

Dear Reader,

Have we got a month of great reading for you! Four very different stories by four talented authors—with, of course, all of the romantic exhilaration you've come to expect from a Harlequin American Romance.

National bestselling author Anne Stuart is back and her fabulous book, *Wild Thing*, will get your heart racing. This is a hero you won't soon forget. This month also continues our HAPPILY WEDDED AFTER promotion with *Special Order Groom*, a delightful reunion story by reader favorite, Tina Leonard.

And let us welcome two new authors to the Harlequin American Romance family. Leanna Wilson, a Harlequin Temptation and Silhouette Romance author, brings us a tender surprise pregnancy book with *Open in Nine Months*. And brand-new author Michele Dunaway makes her sparkling debut with *A Little Office Romance*—get ready to have this bachelor boss hero steal your heart.

Next month we have a whole new look in store for our readers—you'll notice our new covers as well as fantastic promotions such as RETURN TO TYLER and brand-new installments in Muriel Jensen's WHO'S THE DADDY? series. Watch for your favorite authors such as Jule McBride, Judy Christenberry and Cathy Gillen Thacker, all of whom will be back with new books in the coming months.

Wishing you happy reading,

Melissa Jeglinski
Associate Senior Editor
Harlequin American Romance

Open in Nine Months

LEANNA WILSON

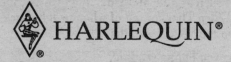

HARLEQUIN®

TORONTO • NEW YORK • LONDON
AMSTERDAM • PARIS • SYDNEY • HAMBURG
STOCKHOLM • ATHENS • TOKYO • MILAN • MADRID
PRAGUE • WARSAW • BUDAPEST • AUCKLAND

For Caroline,
What a joy you are!
I love you more than you will ever know.

ISBN 0-373-16847-0

OPEN IN NINE MONTHS

ABOUT THE AUTHOR

Leanna Wilson believes nothing is better than dreaming up characters and stories and having readers enjoy them as she does. Leanna is the winner of the National Readers' Choice Award and Romance Writers of America's Golden Heart Award. Married to her real-life hero, she lives outside Dallas with their active toddler and newborn. But all the diapers and lullabies haven't kept her from writing. She's busy working on her next book, be it a Silhouette Romance, Harlequin Temptation or Harlequin American Romance novel. She enjoys hearing from readers, so you can write to her c/o: Leanna Wilson, P.O. Box 294227, Lewisville, TX 75029-4277.

Books by Leanna Wilson

HARLEQUIN AMERICAN ROMANCE
847—OPEN IN NINE MONTHS

HARLEQUIN TEMPTATION
763—BACHELOR BLUES

Dear Santa,

I don't want any dolls for Christmas. And I don't need a bike.

Could you please bring me a family?

Love,
Lacey

Chapter One

"You're not Santa Claus."

The tiny voice, full of disappointment, made Joy Chase turn with a start. She stared down at the elfin face. The little girl squinted up at Joy, narrowing her eyes against the bright Colorado sunshine.

Resisting the urge to scratch her face beneath the fake white beard, Joy knelt beside the little girl. Pop's Santa suit pulled tight around her middle. It made the chilly November day feel as warm as July. She didn't often take Pop's place in their hometown's Thanksgiving Day parade, but then Pop didn't usually catch colds, either.

"Can you keep a secret?" Joy asked.

The little girl edged closer, her eyes widening with curiosity. "'Bout what?"

Joy glanced over her shoulder at a group of boys and girls wandering close to the float and kept her voice low. "You can't tell anybody, okay?"

Ebenezer Scrooge didn't have a monopoly on bah-humbug. Those green eyes looked at Joy with an adult-size helping of skepticism. "Sure," the little girl said, "I like secrets."

"Good. You figured it out. I'm not Santa," Joy whispered, deciding honesty was the best tactic. Still, she didn't want to advertise to the other kindergartners playing around the sleigh-shaped float. "Santa caught a cold. And Mrs. Claus insisted he stay in bed. That way he'll be ready to make his journey visiting girls and boys around the world on Christmas Eve."

A smattering of freckles dotted the towheaded girl's nose and cheeks. "I don't believe in Santa. It's just a legend. My mommy told me so."

Joy's heart pinched at the solemn acceptance in the girl's face. Why would any mother burst her daughter's dreams? Santa had never been just a legend to Joy's family. The Christmas season embodied a spirit of giving, a whisper of magic. From the joyous music to the tinsel hanging from a well-shaped evergreen, Joy loved every aspect of the holiday, which was a good thing since her family owned a Christmas store on the downtown corner square of Jingle, Colorado. Every year brought warm memories of Christmas past. This year promised greater anticipation and higher hopes than ever before.

Before she could respond to the little girl's disbelief, a man stepped toward them, effectively blocking the sun and casting a shadow across Joy.

"Lacey." His deep, rumbling voice rolled over Joy like a heat wave, making Pop's Santa suit, with its thick velvet, furry collar and cuffs, as hot and itchy as wearing a wool suit on a beach. A familiarity in his voice made her heart skip a full beat. "Are you bothering Santa?"

''No, Daddy. It's not really—'' Her eyes rounded and she clamped her hand over her mouth. ''Oops.''

Joy gave the little girl a tremulous smile. Trying to take a full breath into her suddenly compressed lungs, she dipped her chin to reach a deep, convincing chuckle. ''It's okay.'' She put her gloved hand on the girl's shoulder and started to rise. ''I was just saying—''

Her gaze collided with the man's smoky stare. She choked. Her throat shut down like a car battery sputtering in the cold. Nearby the high school band began playing ''Santa Claus Is Coming to Town,'' and the trumpets and drums blared too loudly for her to think. But it wasn't the noise or the sudden glare of the sun that made her dizzy. It was the man standing before her.

Oh, God! The ground beneath her feet seemed to teeter and sway. *It's Sam! Sam McCall.* What on earth was *he* doing here?

With his daughter. Then she recognized the little girl he'd called Lacey. She remembered the way he'd pulled his daughter's picture so tenderly out of his wallet, the gentle roughness of his hands, and how her spine tingled, her nerves blazed. As if she'd been transported back seven months in time, she could still hear the catch in his voice as he'd spoken of Lacey. A trembling started in her knees and worked its way up to her heart.

At a quick glance, Sam hadn't changed much since she'd last seen him. Not as much as she had, anyway. Self-consciously, she adjusted her father's wide belt around her middle. Sunlight caught the hint of silvery tones in his brown hair. She remembered the coarse texture of his hair against her fingertips all too well, and she curled her fingers inside Pop's thick gloves, suddenly grateful for the disguise.

Sam looked fit and trim in his tan sheepskin jacket, which made his shoulders look broad enough to cradle her head. His narrow waist put her own to shame. His snug-fitting jeans still had the ability to make her mouth water. His rugged good looks had caught her eye initially. But the pain in his eyes, the sadness in his voice, had drawn her to him. His loneliness had matched her own. She'd understood the longings and needs he'd expressed. They'd found solace in each other's arms. Until she'd snapped out of her trance and headed for home—where she belonged.

But *he* didn't belong here. He was a roamer, a cowboy, on his way to another town, another rodeo, another woman. She'd wanted no part of that lifestyle. When her senses had returned in the harsh light of day, she'd realized her mistake and tiptoed out of the hotel room, never once looking back. Until…

"You were just what?" he asked, interrupting her thoughts and giving her a curious glance that held not an ounce of recognition. Why would he recognize her when she was dressed like a red-coated Pillsbury Doughboy?

"Uh…" She felt as if she'd swallowed her fake beard. Her throat tightened each time she tried to make her voice deeper, emulating Santa, trying to fool Sam. She wondered why he was here. Where was he headed? Cheyenne? Fort Worth? Tucson?

But then she remembered she didn't care. "I was going to ask Lacey if she would be my special elf during the parade."

His gaze slowly shifted toward his daughter. "That ought to be fun." He bent and readjusted Lacey's knit cap. "Right, darlin'?"

Lacey nodded, her solemn green gaze still glued to Joy.

"Are you warm enough?" he asked, zipping his daughter's coat all the way up to her chin.

"Uh-huh." The ball on top of Lacey's cap bobbed like a cork in water.

With her mind reeling and the velvety suit making her perspire, Joy stepped toward the float. "We better get this show on the road." She glanced at the kids scampering around the float. "Come on, my little elves, climb aboard!"

Lacey was the first one to be lifted onto the sleigh. Joy didn't look back at Sam but busied herself gathering a bucket of peppermint candies she would toss to the children along the parade route. Grabbing hold of the edge of the sleigh, Joy struggled to put her foot high enough to hoist herself on board. But her belly bumped the edge and made it nearly impossible to get good leverage. Suddenly a hand settled on her bottom and fingers tightened around her arm. She gasped and jerked away.

And she almost fell right into Sam McCall's arms…again.

She tried to catch her breath. She clutched the float with numb fingers. Blood drained out of her head and pooled in her swollen feet. She was going to faint. Right here on Main Street! That would make twice in the last year. All because of a man. All because Sam had touched her *again!*

"Need a hand up?" the cowboy asked, his tone infinitely more casual than the pounding of her heart.

"Uh..." Her voice squeaked, and she struggled to shift it lower to a more masculine tone. "N-no, thanks. That's all right. I can manage."

His hand remained on her waist, tying her insides up like a Christmas bow. She remembered the firm, smooth planes of his back and the hard muscles along his chest flexing beneath the palm of her hand. Her stomach dropped as it had the first time she'd touched him...the first time he'd kissed her.

Oh, God! Not again!

Dread filled her heart. What if he suddenly discovered the truth of her identity? What if he figured out what she was hiding? Her mind scrambled for what to do, what to say.

"Here," Sam said, refusing to take no for an answer. He hoisted her onto the float with ease. He certainly didn't look ruffled by the chaotic emotions roiling through her. Of course, he thought she was Santa Claus. Or at least a man pretending to be St. Nick. She swallowed a giggle of relief.

She stared down at the tall cowboy. "Thanks."

"Anytime." He gave a tug to the brim of his Stetson. "Just be sure you visit us on Christmas Eve, Santa." He gave her a wink that made her stomach do a slow roll. "I want this Christmas to be the best one Lacey's ever had."

"Me, too," she said, praying they'd spend Christmas far away from her.

"We just moved near here," he said.

Joy felt a cold snap split her spine in two. Had she heard him right? How had this glorious holiday suddenly turned into "The Nightmare Before Christmas"?

"It's been an adjustment," he continued, paying Joy little attention, following his daughter with his steely gaze. Then he leveled Joy with those blue-gray eyes. "Thanks for taking Lacey under your wing. I appreciate it."

Her nerves froze like the icicles hanging from the buildings' eaves along Main Street. The float jolted forward, jarring her insides less than Sam's sudden appearance. Joy's face felt stiff, as if it might break if she tried to smile at the tourists and townsfolk lining the street. Braving the cold weather, they were bundled from head to foot in down jackets, knit caps and fur-lined boots of all colors and sizes. And Joy felt as if she'd just entered the Bermuda Triangle.

"I'll be waiting for you at the end of the parade," Sam called, his voice lifting above the distant sound of the band and the muffled clapping of the crowd.

Joy's heart stopped. Her head snapped around to stare at him, but he was waving at his daughter. Part of her felt a crushing disappointment. No one would be waiting for her. Not this year at least.

Like visions of sugarplums, too many questions danced around her head without answers. Feeling less like she was going to faint and more like she might throw up, she made her way to the top of the sleigh. Arching her back, she leaned her head back and swallowed several times with determination. What was she going to do now?

Should she reveal her identity to Sam before they ran into each other on the street? Jingle was too small a town for her to think she could avoid him for long. *Oh, God!*

She prayed Sam would remember her as well as she remembered every nuance about him. Because she wasn't just an old flame impersonating Santa Claus. She was a pregnant one. Carrying *his* baby!

OVER THE CRUNCH OF ICE as the float moved forward, the bells decorating the fake reindeer and the garbled music the band played a few blocks ahead, Sam heard his daughter call to him. "Daddy! You're 'posed to walk beside us."

"I am?" Sam McCall asked, jogging to catch up to the float as it started to wind its way through town. Then he noticed Mrs. Barnes, the kindergarten teacher, strolling along the other side of the float in her quilted parka, her gray hair wind-tossed, her nose as red as Rudolph's and her glasses half-fogged by the cold, making it difficult for her to navigate.

"Yeah," Lacey said with an enthusiastic grin. "You're 'posed to make sure none of us falls off."

"Okay. Then I won't leave you, darlin'." He positioned himself alongside the float.

Parenting unnerved him. He'd only had full custody of his daughter for less than six months. Each day provided more questions than answers. Most nights, he lay in bed, doubting his abilities and questioning his decision to quit the rodeo circuit. But when he watched Lacey sleeping in her bed at their new ranch, he'd felt a peace he'd never known, and the questions and doubts dissolved beneath the intense love he felt for his daughter.

In an attempt to be an involved father, not just a sideline dad, he'd volunteered to help on this school field trip. It had solved his dilemma about what to do on Thanksgiving, since he doubted he could have cooked an edible turkey, much less a pecan pie.

Now he once again questioned his sanity. One kid was hard enough to watch. A class full of squirming five-year-olds seemed impossible. A herd of ornery cows stampeding across the plains seemed easier. Already a headache pounded in his temples.

Eyeing the kids lining the float like he would a rank, unpredictable bull, he motioned for one daredevil to move back a step. All he needed was for one to fall. Then Sam's gaze collided with the jolly old elf sitting on top of the red sleigh. He sensed the old fellow watching him, observing him. Did Santa doubt his ability, too?

The rotund, red-suited elf diverted his gaze and slapped the reins against the fake reindeer's backs. ''On Dasher, on Comet...'' Santa tossed a handful of peppermints to the crowd and chuckled, ''Ho, ho, ho.'' But a frown pinched the skin between those two bushy white brows that couldn't possibly be real. Maybe Santa had a headache, too.

As the afternoon waned, Sam busied himself wiping chilled noses, retying kids' hoods and finding missing mittens along the parade route. By the time their float reached the town square and came to a final halt, he felt like a rubber band pulled in twelve directions.

One by one, he lifted Lacey's classmates off the

float. They made a mad dash toward Santa, who handed out peppermint sticks. Old St. Nick bent down to their level, giving each one a pat on the back and a "Have a merry Christmas!"

"Daddy!" Lacey called, running up to him, her cheeks reddened with the cold. "Can we go to the party at Santa's workshop?"

He hadn't seen her this excited since they'd moved to the western side of the state and taken up residence in a rundown ranch that Sam was renovating and restocking with registered cattle. Transformed by the sweet pleasure on his daughter's face, he said, "Sure, darlin'. Why don't you go tell everyone to line up and we'll head right over?"

As she scampered off, Sam shifted his gaze back to Santa and edged closer. "I owe you."

Santa's bright blue eyes widened. He straightened, arched his back, making his padded belly strain against the wide black belt. "For what?"

Sam shrugged. "For somehow making Lacey excited about Christmas. So far, getting her interested in the holiday has been like pulling teeth."

Santa tilted his head and the fluffy ball at the end of his red cap plopped to the side. "How come?" He shuttered his gaze, then said in a deep, husky voice, "Sorry. That's none of my business."

Santa started to turn away, but Sam needed this man who obviously had experience working with children. If Santa, even a fake one, couldn't help, then Sam didn't know who could.

"It's my fault," Sam confessed, feeling the brunt of his words like a blow to his own heart. He'd lost so much time already. But not anymore. Something in Santa's eyes softened and made Sam want to share the burden he'd carried for so long. "I want to make this Christmas magical for her, to make up for lost time. But she doesn't seem interested."

That's enough, McCall. Don't spill your guts to this stranger. Santa doesn't care. Embarrassed by how much he'd revealed, he dug the toe of his boot into a wedge of icy snow caked on the sidewalk.

"That's a heavy burden to carry. I wish you luck."

Sam gave the brim of his hat a jerk, pulling it down to cover the burning sensation in his cheeks. "Well, thanks for whatever you did."

Santa gave Sam a brief smile that had the edges of his beard pulling loose at the corners. "I didn't do anything."

The jolly old elf's voice had the timbre of a saxophone and gave Sam an odd sensation along his spine. This St. Nick easily reminded him of the storybook he'd once read to Lacey. But there was something else, something familiar about him. The bearded Santa had a round belly, rosy cheeks and a pair of sparkling blue eyes that looked...

Sam shook his head. The altitude must be getting to him. Or the cold, which seemed to cut right through his bones. He crossed his arms over his chest and took another step closer, eyeing Santa more thoroughly. "You know, I've been thinking that I know you somehow."

The vivid blue eyes grew round with what looked like concern. He took a step back.

"Of course! I'm Santa Claus."

Sam chuckled. What did he expect? Santa to

shake hands and state his real name in front of all these kids who were lining up beside the float like little tin soldiers? Lowering his voice, he added, "But underneath this getup, you look...familiar. Maybe it's your voice."

"You run into many white-bearded fat men often?"

That's when Sam noticed an errant lock of coppery hair curlicuing along Santa's nape. Curious, he watched the jolly elf fumble with the bucket of peppermints, his hands covered with oversize black gloves. After a nervous moment, Santa shifted from boot to boot, adjusting his belt and patting his long white beard. The thick white mustache pulled away from the corner of his mouth. Sam watched Santa's lips stretch into a frown. A decidedly, at closer range, feminine-shaped mouth!

Sam smiled at his discovery. A woman, eh? No wonder he...she was nervous. He'd gotten too close. She didn't want anyone to know she wasn't the real Santa Claus, much less a woman. He glanced at the padded figure, remembered the smooth shape beneath the palm of his hand when he'd helped to lift him...her onto the float. Suddenly his senses confirmed that there were definitely female curves beneath all that red velvet.

All in all, she didn't make a bad Santa. He'd seen worse-dressed look-alikes whose cotton beards hung limp and whose bellies had the discernible square shape of a pillow. At least this lady had a good costume. It took careful inspection to figure out this Santa was a fake.

With a wry smile, he doubted she looked like the

ancient elf out of costume. His roving eye scrutinized the bulging Santa suit from the furry collar down to the shiny black boots as he tried to envision what she would look like without her glued-on beard or without that padded suit.

"You're not a traditional Kris Kringle," he said, keeping his voice low. "Maybe we should call you Kristy Kringle."

Abruptly she turned away. Intrigued, he moved closer, trapping her against the float. "I'm Sam. Sam McCall." He dropped his voice to a controlled whisper, careful not to let the boys and girls nearby hear him. "And you're a woman."

"Very observant, Sherlock." Her voice rose to a higher pitch, a more feminine tone. Her rosy cheeks brightened, and she lifted a frosted brow, daring him to blow her cover. "Let's make it our little secret." Her voice shifted to a husky, intimate whisper that made him think of rumpled bedsheets and shot liquid heat through his veins.

A twinge of guilt tweaked his conscience. What was he doing? Flirting with Santa? He shook that notion loose. Ridiculous. What had gotten into him?

Altitude. Definitely the altitude.

It didn't matter, anyway. He didn't have time for romance. Not with a new ranch that required work and a daughter who desperately needed his attention.

Maybe it had been too long since he'd been with a woman. No, that was too easy. The simple fact was he hadn't wanted another woman, not since he'd met Joy. Not since she'd walked out on him. His shoulders bunched with irritation. After that escapade, he'd written off women. He didn't need them. They were trouble. He'd learned his lesson.

"I have work to do," she said in a voice as cool as a Colorado breeze.

"Sure." He backed up, irritated at himself.

Ignoring him, she turned on the heel of her boot and addressed the children waiting in line. "Okay, my little elves." Her voice dropped again, covering her femininity. But this time, he wasn't fooled. This time, her voice sounded incredibly sexy, like warm honey. "How would you like some punch and cookies and a chance to tell your Christmas wish to Santa—" her gaze shifted to Sam, then she corrected herself "—I mean, me?"

"Yeah!" the kids cried in unison.

"Then follow along."

Falling in line with his daughter, Sam walked the short distance to Santa's Workshop. It was an old store nestled between the library and a barbershop. The bricks were a rusty red, but the trim had been painted bright green. In the windows tiny white lights twinkled merrily and a colored wreath decorated the door that squeaked as Santa opened it.

He took his daughter's hand in his, focusing on Lacey, forgetting about any temptations that might distract him from what was really important.

"LACEY, COME ON UP HERE." Joy patted her tired thigh. The little girl had been lurking at the back of her family's store all afternoon while the other kids took their turns climbing on Santa's lap. She remembered what Sam had said about his daughter, and she wanted to help. As much as she could, without getting involved.

Head down, hands clasped behind her back, Lacey shuffled toward her. Sam squeezed his daughter's shoulder and gave her a smile that should have made any child beam. Reaching down, Joy helped Lacey crawl into her lap. After settling her into place, Joy looked into a pair of doleful eyes that reminded her of the longing she'd once seen in Sam's. Dismissing the pinching of her heart as overactive hormones, she focused on Lacey and ignored Sam.

"Did you like the cookies and punch?" Joy asked, hoping to cheer up the little girl.

"Yes, sir." Still no smile, no light in the girl's eyes.

"How about the parade? Wasn't that fun?"

"Uh-huh." But she looked more dejected than thrilled.

Unable to lift the gloom from the little girl's solemn face, Joy felt her own brow tightening with a frown. "Was it your first parade?"

Again, she nodded, but this time remained silent.

Joy's gaze met Sam's briefly, but the connection seemed instantaneous, as if an electrical current had zapped her. Shifting Lacey on her lap, uncomfortable with her reaction to Sam, worried that he'd see through her disguise, she twisted slightly away from Sam's intense gaze. "Are you ready to tell me what you want for Christmas?"

Slowly Lacey shook her head from side to side. Her bottom lip suddenly quivered.

Lifting the little girl's chin, Joy felt a stab of pain

in her own heart. She wanted to wrap her arms around Lacey and cuddle her close. Instead, she settled a reassuring arm around the little girl's narrow shoulders, tucking her snugly against her side. "Why not?"

Lacey shrugged.

"Do you know what you want?"

The little girl sniffed. "Yeah."

"Are you keeping it a secret?"

"Nope."

"Why won't you tell me then?"

"Won't do no good. That's all." Lacey's hopeless voice made Joy's heart ache.

Lowering her voice so none of the other children could hear, Joy whispered, "I know I said I'm not the real Santa, but he listens to me. I can let Santa know what you want."

"I prayed, like Daddy taught me, but it didn't do no good."

Understanding twisted Joy's heart. How well she remembered her own prayers as a child, asking God to bring back her mommy, promising to be good, begging for a whole family. Feeling as helpless as a doctor treating cancer with a lollipop, Joy asked, "Isn't there anything you'd like Santa to bring you?"

Lacey remained silent for a long time, pursing her lips and wrinkling her forehead. "A new tree."

Surprised, Joy asked, "What kind?"

"A great big green one. Tall as the ceiling. Daddy bought a silver one. And it's teeny-tiny. We had to put it on the table. And it wobbles. It don't smell like a real tree." She looped her arm over Joy's shoulder and whispered, "Daddy tried. But he's kinda new to all this."

"I see." She glanced at Sam over his daughter's blond ponytail. He was watching them, trying to discern what they were saying. His firm brow knitted into a frown, drawing his straight brows down toward the bridge of his nose.

"Could you help?" Lacey asked with reserved hope.

"I think so." Joy offered the little girl a tender smile.

"Thanks!" Lacey hugged her, planted a wet kiss on her cheek and jumped down to play with her friends.

Joy's heart pounded, echoing the headache pummeling her temples. She couldn't get involved in the little girl's life without becoming entangled once again with the father. And she didn't need that. She had enough worries of her own. And Sam was one of them.

What was she going to do about him? She had no choice, really. She'd watched Sam all day with the group of kindergartners, holding their hands, wiping away tears, cleaning up spilled punch and picking up broken cookies. He had a tender side, a gentle way with kids that moved her, made her wonder what he'd be like as a daddy to their baby. But that always stopped her.

She didn't want a daddy for her baby...or a husband for her. She was perfectly happy to raise her child alone. After all, she didn't love Sam. And he didn't love her. She would never settle for anything less in marriage.

Could she deprive her child of having a father? Guilt twisted inside her for not telling Sam about the baby. He had a right to know. But he already had his hands full. She didn't want a man feeling obligated to help her. No, she couldn't tell him. Not yet. Not until she thought about the situation more.

First things first. She had to tell him who she was. But how? And when?

"It's time for us to be off," Sam said, jarring her out of her thoughts.

"Oh! Already?"

"It's getting late. Some of the kids live out in the boondocks. It'll take a while to get them home."

"You've certainly got a handful now. All sugared up and ready to go."

"Not a problem. I'll just hog-tie 'em if they get to be too much." He gave her a wink that had her pulse fluttering. He leaned close, and she caught a whiff of his subtle yet overwhelmingly masculine cologne. It made her nerves stand on end. "Mind telling me what Lacey asked for?"

"What?" Joy asked, her brain foggy from his nearness.

"I've been trying to find out what she wants for Christmas, but her lips are closed tighter than a spring trap."

"Oh!" Joy's cheeks flamed. "She asked for a new Christmas tree. A great big green one, to be precise. She mentioned something about a pathetic silver one at home."

This time, his ears turned a dusty red. "Oh, that. It's like the tree I had as a kid. I thought she'd like the pretty colors. It turns around and everything. But

I guess it's not much to look at. I don't have much in the way of Christmas decorations. Maybe you could help us pick out some things.''

His thick, rich voice made her think of melting chocolate kisses. Or maybe she was just having another craving. For food. Not Sam. ''Uh, well...''

''You have a nice store here, but with all these kids, I haven't had a chance to look around much. Could you help us?''

How could she say no? But how could she agree? Her insides shifted restlessly. What else could she do? ''Sure, I can.''

''Like I said, I want to make this Christmas extra special. So whatever it takes.'' His gunmetal-gray eyes shot her with a load of emotion she hadn't anticipated. His distress touched a tender, vulnerable spot in her heart. At the same time it made her quake in her boots. She had to steel herself against Sam McCall, not fall victim to her own emotions and his charm again.

''I'm sure you'll do a fine job.''

He shrugged, making his shoulders seem even wider than she remembered. He started to turn.

''Uh, Sam—'' Her gaze shifted toward the kids milling around the store. She couldn't just take off her beard and reveal herself. The kids, all except for Lacey, thought she was Santa. ''Why don't you come by tomorrow? Any time is fine.''

The corner of his mouth lifted in a sexy smile, pinching a crease in the flat plane of his tanned cheek. ''Okay. We'll be here.'' Again, he turned, then looked back at her. His eyes softened to a misty silver that had her heart turning a somersault. ''If this helps my daughter, then I'll be grateful to you...."

His pause pressured her to supply her name. But she resisted. This wasn't the time, not with a store full of squirming kids. "Just call me Santa's li'l helper."

When she would have backed away, he put his hand on her arm. She felt a fluttering in her belly. His mercurial gaze shifted to her mouth, and her temperature went up a degree or two. A tingling started in the pit of her stomach and spread through her limbs. He took a step closer, and her breath caught in her chest. She had a sudden inexplicable need to be kissed. By Sam.

It was ridiculous.

It was insane.

But it was honest. Too honest for her own good!

God, she remembered their first kiss. He'd caught her by surprise. She'd been about to leave after they'd shared a nice, quiet dinner. It had only been their first date. But it had felt as if they'd known each other forever. The cab had already pulled to the curb and was waiting for her. But they'd lingered, reluctant to say goodbye. Then Sam had pulled her slowly against him, dipped his head and captured her mouth...and heart.

Even now, seven months later, she felt a fiery heat blaze inside her. It had been the most intense kiss she'd ever experienced. And the most rewarding.

Reaching out now, he touched the corner of her mouth, jolting her back to the present and sending pulsing tremors down her spine. Her stomach tumbled over itself as her heart beat its way to her throat. *Oh, God! He was going to kiss her. Right here! In the store! And she was going to let him!*

Did he know who she was? Had he figured it out? Or, heaven help her, did he pick up women this easily all the time? She'd fallen for him so fast, like a rock sliding down the side of a mountain. She'd thought she could resist that pull, but gravity seemed too strong to fight. She had to be stronger. She had to resist. The thought of him attracting other women as easily as his magic had worked on her felt like an ice cube shimmying down her spine. She stiffened and took a decisive step backward.

"Hold still," he whispered, his voice trapping her more securely than brute force. He pressed his thumb against her thick white mustache and touched it to the corner of her mouth. "You were coming apart."

She was coming apart...at the seams. Wanting what she shouldn't. Needing him like a crazy woman.

A few minutes later, she basked in the quiet of her empty store, clomped to the front in Pop's over-size boots and swiveled the sign around in the window to read Closed. Sighing, she went back to the checkout counter, eased her tired frame onto the stool and felt the soft stirrings of her baby.

Automatically, she laid a hand on her belly, cherishing this sweet time with her baby nestled safely inside her. Remembering Sam, she felt herself tense with doubts and questions. Heat flashed like a beacon inside her.

"I can't stand to wear this one second longer."

She started to peel off the beard, wincing as it tugged on sensitive flesh.

She'd been careless and stupid with Sam once before. She wouldn't let it happen again. She had to keep up her guard. Tomorrow she'd reveal her true identity. She couldn't keep that a secret. Later she'd decide whether he should know the baby was his. And she promised herself she'd use intellect rather than her heart.

As she tossed the white beard and mustache on the counter she began to hum a lullaby to her baby. The tiny flutters and abrupt kicks never ceased to amaze her at the miracle growing inside her. It made her long for her mother and at the same time feel connected to her again. It was a bond that could not be broken, even by death, and it moved Joy in ways she'd never imagined, made her throat close at the bottled-up emotions.

Suddenly the door to the shop swung open, and an out-of-breath Sam raced inside. Joy gasped and lunged for the beard lying on the counter. But it was too late.

"Did you find some mittens—" He came to an abrupt halt. His eyes narrowed, then widened with comprehension. "Joy?"

The blood in her veins froze like icicles. *Oh, God!*

Sam took a hesitant step forward, his movement awkward, jarring. She took an automatic step backward and put her hands protectively over Pop's wide belt buckle that partially covered her bulging belly.

"Is that you?" he rasped.

She couldn't find her voice. Her knees felt as if the glue in her joints had melted beneath a sudden heat wave. *My stars! What do I do now?*

Chapter Two

Reality walloped Sam with a hard punch to the gut. Sam stared at Joy's heart-shaped face, sun-kissed, freckled features, pert nose and sensuous mouth. And he remembered a soft spring night that had turned hot and sultry with one kiss from her.

What the hell was she doing here dressed up like Santa Claus? He gawked at her getup, which hid those sensuous curves he remembered so well beneath the red velvet padded costume.

She took an unsteady breath, and her hand clutched the fake white beard as if she'd strangled it to death. "At least you remembered."

How could I have forgotten?

No wonder he'd been attracted to her all bundled up in that Santa costume. No wonder he'd noticed her eyes! Irritated at his reaction to her, angry at her deception, he demanded, "Why didn't you say who you were earlier?"

A red hue stole up her neck and spread across her cheeks, brightening her eyes to laser points. She crossed her arms over her chest. "What'd you want me to say? 'Hey, kids, look who's here. A one-night stand from my past!'''

A vibrating awareness pulsated between them. That one night, they'd seemed so close, not just physically, but in a way that rarely happened to a man and woman. It had seemed as if their very souls had kissed. Ah, hell, they'd just been lonely. Nothing more.

He should have known better. *Once burned, McCall, makes you skittish as a green colt. Twice makes you look like an idiot. Three times certifies you as a damn fool.*

And he was. Because, like a fool, he'd wanted to fall asleep next to Joy more than just once. He'd wanted, needed more than one passionate night.

The distance between them now felt as chilly and remote as Pike's Peak. Anger rolled over him like a boulder tumbling down a mountainside, crushing his memories with the cold reality of her leaving him that following morning. Without even a goodbye or hastily written note.

"What are you doing here?" Irritation tightened his voice.

She flinched. "I work here…live here. I always have. This is the place I told you about."

He felt as if ice water had been tossed in his face. Now it made sense. No wonder he'd had a feeling that he'd been to Jingle. She'd told him of her hometown lovingly…longingly described every block along the town square, the quaint buildings and friendly neighbors. Something inside him must have recognized it instantly. Damn! Had he unconsciously come looking for her? A cold sweat popped out on his brow.

No. Hell, no!

He had no use for women. Especially a woman like Joy who'd used him and left—exactly the way his ex-wife had.

"You talked like you didn't live here," he said, trying to recall her exact words, but that night seemed so long ago. He wanted to forget it. So much had happened since then; his concern for Lacey consumed his every waking thought. But at night, in his dreams, he remembered.

Damn her.

Damn him for not being able to erase her from his mind.

JOY SHRUGGED. She didn't owe him any explanations. She'd gone a little crazy for a week or two. She'd turned twenty-nine back in April. Twenty-nine was hard enough for most single women, but it had put her face-to-face with questions she hadn't wanted to answer. She'd been thrown into a tailspin of self-evaluation. She'd gone through a difficult period.

"So, I guess you didn't come here looking for me." She propped a hand on her hip, trying to tease him, but her joke fell flat. She hadn't expected him to find her—on purpose or otherwise. Still, a margin of disappointment sifted through her. He hadn't been looking for her.

His gray eyes flashed like white lightning. He shoved his hands into his pockets. "Why would I after the way you left?"

Guilt stung her. "I shouldn't have treated you that way. For that I apologize. I just…" How could she explain the way she'd felt? How fear had overwhelmed her? Waking beside him, she'd realized she wanted what her parents had—love, commitment, the till-death-do-you-part kind. How could she have ever found that with a cowboy like Sam who lived out of a duffel bag and who'd never known a true home?

"What is it you want then?" His granite voice sounded hard and cold. "Why'd you volunteer to help us with our Christmas?"

His implication made her body tremble with suppressed rage. She felt the baby stir inside her, punch a little fist into her rib cage, a reminder that they shared more now than one overwhelming passion-filled night. Grateful she hadn't had time to remove the oversize red velvet jacket before Sam had barged back into her shop, she fiddled with the white furry fringe.

"You make it sound like I planned this whole thing. Like I put on this outfit, knowing you were coming here. Out of the blue, I might add. So I could be waiting to pounce on you. Yep, you found me out. Of course, how I got you to ask for my help took some manipulation, but then I'm sure you have an answer for that, too."

He quirked an eyebrow at her toxic response. "Okay, you couldn't have expected me. Any more than I planned to find you. But why agree to help?"

That gave her pause. Again her baby moved. "I empathized with Lacey. I understand what it's like not to have a mom."

"She has a mother." His tone was quick and cutting like a razor. "Just not a very good one. Besides, she has me now. I can give my daughter whatever she needs."

"Can you?"

His venomous look made Joy swallow hard. She should have kept her mouth shut. The emptiness left by her mother's untimely death had never been filled, no matter how hard her father had tried. A little girl needed a mother and father. Maybe she'd voiced her own doubts about parenting this baby alone. Was she depriving her own child by keeping the father in the dark?

"I'm sorry, Sam. I didn't mean anything when I agreed to help. Believe me, I was going to tell you tomorrow who I was. I knew I couldn't hide behind this costume for long." But how long could she hide her bulging belly?

"I understand if you want to find someone else to help you with Christmas. After all, it is awkward." Here was her chance. "But you should know…"

She faltered, needing more time to be certain telling him was the right choice. Things had happened too fast. She couldn't think straight. Had he changed from the roaming cowboy, the man more accustomed to the road than a home? Would he make a good daddy for her baby?

"Look." He made the decision for her. "Back in Denver you and I connected. We clicked. If only for a little while. But I'm not interested in pursuing a relationship. I've got all I can handle right now. Okay?"

His words cut her to the quick. Her spine stiffened. She wasn't looking for a handout.

"I brought Lacey here to settle down," he continued, "to make a home. I was hoping to have a traditional Christmas. She came to live with me…right after…" His gaze burned into Joy.

Anger swelled inside her like storm clouds brewing. She fidgeted with the wide brass belt buckle at her thickened waist, and kept her mouth shut. She didn't need or want any more reminders of that one night with Sam. All she had to do was fall asleep and the memories of his kiss, his touch, poured through her mind like sweet, intoxicating wine.

"I've been a roamer for so long that it's a difficult transition for both of us. But we'll manage. I'll figure out a way to explain to Lacey why you can't help."

Joy's chest tightened as she thought of the little girl's need for a real Christmas. She remembered her own disappointments as a child. Her father working late, her mother's fatal automobile accident. She felt a heavy weight inside her. "I'm sure you will."

She knew then she'd keep her secret to herself. Maybe she'd judged him wrong in the past. Maybe she'd underestimated him…and herself. She'd labeled him irresponsible, unable to settle down. But now he was a dedicated father, trying to build a home and family.

Remorse squeezed Joy's chest for all that might have been. If only she hadn't been so scared, so frightened of the passion they'd shared together, so terrified of losing a part of herself. Now it was too late. Sam had all he could handle. She didn't want to shackle him with more responsibilities. She and her child would make do on their own.

Automatically she laid a hand on her belly, felt the baby nestled safely inside her. Aware of Sam studying her, she let her hand fall to her side. "Well, then," she said, wondering how they'd end this for good, "maybe—"

"Daddy!" Lacey raced through the door, her cheeks reddened from the cold. "Mrs. Barnes said we need to—" She stopped in her tracks and stared up at Joy. "You're a girl!"

Managing a warm chuckle, Joy nodded. "Just like you."

The little girl blinked as she took in the surprise. "That's cool. Can I purtend to be Santa, too?"

"Maybe an elf, darlin'," Sam said, ruffling the knit ball at the top of his daughter's cap. "Are all the kids on the bus?"

Lacey nodded. "Mrs. Barnes is ready to go. Did you find Tommy's glove?"

"Uh…" Sam paused, glancing around. "Not yet."

"There it is." Lacey skipped over to the counter and picked up the red glove off the floor. "See you tomorrow, Mrs. Santa." She began to giggle.

"You can call me Joy." She walked to the other side of the counter and secured the girl's scarf around her exposed neck. Her gaze collided with Sam's. He expected her to back out of their deal. To be the bad guy. Her heart contracted. "Lacey, I'm not sure we'll be able to…"

Lacey shifted her gaze to her daddy, her eyes widening, filling with sudden tears. "She won't help us?"

"It's not that, darlin'." He knelt beside her. "It's—"

"But, Daddy, she's got all this Christmas stuff. She knows how to fix things up and make 'em look all sparkly. She can—"

"Lacey, Santa, er, Joy is busy. She has a store to run. We'll manage just fine. You and me, kiddo."

"But Daddy…" Lacey turned her watery gaze on Joy again.

Joy's chest tightened as if a vise squeezed it. Sam's desperate gaze landed on her, too, pleaded silently with her. But what was he asking? For her to disappoint Lacey? Or for her to come to the rescue? Confused, she struggled to resist caving in to her roiling emotions. "It shouldn't take too much time."

"Yippee!" Lacey gave her a beatific smile that warmed Joy from the inside out like a cup of hot cocoa. "See you tomorrow!" She grabbed her daddy's hand and pulled him toward the door.

Before he left, he glanced over his shoulder and mouthed "Thank you."

So she'd made the right decision. Or had she?

Before the door of her shop closed behind them, a cold blast of Colorado air tumbled inside, making her shiver with dread. She had another day to think about her decision. But would twenty-four hours make a difference? She doubted anything would change her mind. How would she keep Sam from knowing she was pregnant? And that he was the father of her child?

"WASN'T SHE PRETTY, DADDY?"

"Hmm?" Sam turned away from the stove and the hamburger patties sizzling in the frying pan.

Lacey sat at their makeshift kitchen table, actually a card table he'd bought at a garage sale, and colored a Christmas picture. The drawing clearly reminded him of what she wanted—a perfect Christmas with all the trimmings and decorations. Everything she deserved. He wanted to give her a magical Christmas. But how?

"Santa," she said, not looking up from her task. "I mean, Joy. Isn't she pretty?"

Yeah, too pretty for his own good. He tried to block the image of Joy's sparkling blue eyes from his mind. "I suppose."

"I wish I looked like her." With her head bent, Lacey worked her hand up and down as she drew a green triangle-shaped tree on construction paper.

"I think you're a lot prettier," he stated with conviction. He walked across the kitchen, his boots scuffing the hardwood floor, and dropped a kiss on the top of his daughter's head.

His heart squeezed with parental pride. He'd helped bring this guileless creature into the world. Well, okay, he admitted, he hadn't done any of the hard work. He'd been out on the road, as usual, trying to make a buck to pay for the expensive crib and baby clothes Lacey's mother had bought for their daughter. He'd missed her birth. He'd missed a lot of things. But not anymore.

His daughter glanced up at him and gave him a dimpled smile that always had the power to charm him. "I like her. Don't you?"

"Hmm." He tried to hedge the question. He didn't want to think about Joy Chase anymore.

"She's nice." Lacey shifted in her seat, hooking a leg under her bottom to raise herself higher. "You know what?"

"What?" He matched her smile with one of his own, hoping she might change the topic.

"She told me first thing that she weren't Santa."

"Wasn't Santa," he automatically corrected her, as his ex-wife had often corrected him. Then a chilly sensation rippled down his spine. "What? She told you that?" He crossed his arms over his chest, irritation sparking inside him. What exactly had Joy said? "When, baby?"

She blinked at him as if stunned by the sudden anger sharpening his tone. "When we got there this morning. It's okay, Daddy. I already knowed that."

"Knowed…" His thoughts spun and he gave himself a mental shake. "Knew what?"

She gave an exasperated sigh. "That she wasn't Santa. Mommy told me there isn't such a thing as Santa Claus or the Easter Bunny."

Anger snapped inside him. Why had his ex-wife spoiled all their child's fantasies? His hand closed into a fist. He remembered a night not so long ago when he'd sneaked into his daughter's room, removed the tiny white tooth from beneath her pillow and replaced it with a crisp dollar bill. Now Lacey's confession twisted that memory like a painful spike in his heart. Every little girl deserved to believe in fairy tales. And his ex-wife had stolen that from Lacey.

"What about the tooth fairy?" he asked, trying to keep a lighter tone.

"Uh-oh." Lacey's green eyes widened, as if she'd been caught with her hand in the cookie jar. Solemnly she nodded. "Does that mean I won't get no more money when I lose another tooth?"

He laughed. "Depends on if you start believing real quick."

She giggled. "Okay, I believe." She turned her attention back to her drawing, choosing a red crayon to draw circles on the tree. "When I told her I knowed she wasn't Santa, you know what she said?"

The woman had captured his daughter's attention. Just as she'd snagged Sam's several months earlier. He'd tried to shrug off the spell she'd cast over him, but it hadn't been easy. How would he handle his daughter's infatuation with Joy? Wishing they could get off the subject of Joy, he quirked a questioning brow at his daughter and waited for her to continue.

"She said I was smart." Lacey beamed, then tilted her head to the side. "But I didn't know she was a girl. Did you, Daddy?"

He shook his head, his mind tripping over his daughter's words.

"I thought she looked all round and cuddly like my teddy bear in her red suit." Lacey's brow furrowed with concern. "Do you think she's really fat? Like my teacher, Mrs. Barnes?"

"Um, no. I don't think she's fat." A flash of a memory surfaced of Joy snuggled next to him, warm and naked, with skin as smooth as a satin negligee and a body that could shame any Victoria's Secret model. The image made his insides burn, made his heart yearn. But he doused those flames of desire with a bucket of reality. Joy was just like his ex-wife. She'd walked out on him. Without an explanation. Without a goodbye. Leaving him with a cold emptiness resonating inside his chest.

"How do you know?" Lacey asked, her curiosity making him nervous.

"I don't know. Just a guess. Most folks dressing up as Santa need extra padding beneath their red suits." Again his mind played tricks on him, conjured up images he should forget, red-hot images that made him wonder what exactly Joy had been wearing under that Santa suit.

"Oh." His daughter lifted her head, sniffed and wrinkled her nose. "Daddy, dinner's burning again."

"Damn." He jogged back to the stove. Already he could smell the acrid smoke rising from the skillet. Grabbing the lid off the frying pan, he yelped. It fell to the counter with a clank. Reaching for a hot pad and spatula to turn the hamburger patties that sizzled and popped grease across the stovetop, he maneuvered the skillet off the burner and saved most of the burgers.

"Did you burn yourself, Daddy?" Lacey stared up at him with such innocence that his chest ached.

No, he thought, Joy had. And he hated to admit how much she'd hurt him. But no woman would hurt him again. "I'm okay."

Or he would be as soon as he got Joy out of their lives.

SAM DEBATED ALL NIGHT about taking Lacey back to Joy's shop. But it was the only Christmas store for miles around. And he'd promised his daughter.

Years ago he'd made a pact with himself. He'd never lie to Lacey, never break a promise and never leave her as others had left him. That conviction put him on the road toward Jingle and Joy's Christmas shop.

Lacey sat beside him in the truck, her seat belt fastened snugly across her lap. She stared quietly out the window, looking at the snow-tipped pine trees lining the narrow, winding road. Sam struggled with how to prepare his daughter for the fact that this was a one-time encounter with Joy. After today, they were on their own. He'd somehow make Lacey a rip-snortin' holiday. If it killed him.

"Here comes Santa Claus..." Lacey began singing, her high-pitched voice making him smile.

Letting his mind drift, he hummed along while he manuevered the truck across an ice-patched bridge.

"Don't you know the words, Daddy?"

He shrugged, feeling as if his sheepskin jacket had suddenly shrunk two sizes. "Uh...yeah, I guess."

"How come you don't sing it with me?"

"Well, I..." He didn't have a reason. His life had hardly been a Broadway musical, for God's sake. He'd had a father who preferred spending time with his drinking buddies than with his son. If his old man had ever sung to Sam it would have been a Hank Williams crying-in-your-beer song. And hell, Sam couldn't even remember his mother, much less if she'd ever sung a lullabye or Christmas carol.

"We sing all the time at school. I don't think Mrs. Barnes knows she can't sing too good."

Sam chuckled. "Why don't you teach me one of the songs you've learned?"

Lacey grinned. "Okay!" She shifted in her seat so she could watch him instead of the dark line of snow-banked clouds moving in from the west. "Do you know this one?" She started singing, "On the first day of Christmas my true love gave to me…"

Soon they reached Jingle, a much sleepier town the day after Thanksgiving. With the parade over, a smaller crowd milled from store to store, carrying Christmas packages beneath their arms. Already Lacey had sung the same Christmas carol eight times. Sam's head began to ache when he pulled in front of the shop.

Hand in hand, they walked across the crunchy snow-packed sidewalk. Sam pushed open the door and heard the jingle of the bell above his head. He scanned the front of the store but didn't see Joy anywhere in sight. The tension along his shoulders eased a notch, as if he'd been given a reprieve. He doffed his Stetson and helped Lacey remove her mittens and cap.

"I'll be right with you," Joy called.

At the sound of her voice, a heater seemed to click on inside him. "No hurry."

"Oh!" Joy popped up from behind the front counter. Her face was red with exertion or embarrassment, which made her eyes shine like a clear summer sky. She pushed back an unruly strand of curly red hair that had fallen across her forehead and settled a bulky wool sweater over her hips. "You're here."

"I told you we would be."

"Hi!" Lacey skipped over to the counter and stared up at her new hero. "What are we gonna buy first?"

Joy laughed. Her smile was as dazzling as pure gold. "My kind of girl. Always ready to do some shopping."

Great, Sam thought. He was going to go broke in one afternoon. But if it made his daughter happy, he'd willingly turn over all his savings and start over from scratch.

"What do you think you need first, Lacey?"

"A tree." She bounced on the balls of her feet.

"We can't get that here, darlin'." Sam wished he'd taken her somewhere else. Already his insides churned as he avoided looking at Joy and tried to forget all they'd shared.

"But you can get decorations for the tree here," Joy added. "Then I'll show you where you can buy the best tree."

"A green one?" Lacey asked.

"Of course." Joy's gaze shifted to Sam. "I guess I should have asked about your budget first. Do you want to buy decorations or make them instead?"

"Both!" Lacey said with an enthusiasm he hadn't witnessed in the last few months.

A sudden surge of gratefulness made him forget this woman couldn't be counted on. Almost.

"Why don't we start with things you'll need to buy?" Joy said, glancing over Lacey's head toward Sam. "Do you want some lights for the tree?"

"Can we, Daddy?"

"Sure." He twirled his cowboy hat in his hands, not sure what to do with himself, feeling totally out of his element. "What color?"

"Red and white and green..." Lacey rolled the toe of her tennis shoe inward. "And yellow and blue. But not purple. That's not a Christmas color." She looked up at Joy then. "Is it?"

"Not usually." She leaned her hip against the counter, folding her arms just under her breasts, which seemed fuller than he remembered. He jerked his thoughts back to his daughter and the Christmas he was going to provide her. "But this is *your* tree, Lacey, so you can have any color. Even pink."

"Pink!" Lacey giggled. "That'd be silly."

"Maybe," Joy agreed with a conspiratorial smile and a wink that had Sam's blood pressure rising. "Tree lights are along aisle four. You'll find chaser lights, ones that play music as they blink on and off, or plain ones. I need to find a special order. But if you have any questions—"

The shop door opened, and Sam felt a cold draft at his back.

"Joy, my true love," a male voice sang to the tune Lacey had taught Sam earlier.

Turning, Sam flicked his gaze over a tall, lanky gentleman with a shock of blond hair and smiling brown eyes. Instantly Sam felt his spine turn as brittle as an icicle.

"Hi, Charlie," Joy said. "What can I do for you today?"

"Marry me."

Sam's gaze snapped back to see a blush rise along Joy's neck and stain her cheeks.

"Now, Charlie, you know I can't. I'm booked solid today."

Shaking his head, the man stamped his feet on the rug by the door and walked toward the counter. He glanced at Sam and said, "She turns me down daily. But I haven't given up hope yet." He leaned across the counter and gave Joy a peck on the cheek. "You're looking pretty today, my love. How are you feeling?"

"Uh..." Her eyes widened. "Fine. I'm fine." Her gaze ping-ponged between Sam and Charlie, finally landing back on Sam. "Those lights are in aisle four."

Charlie turned toward him then. "Are you new in town?" He stuck out his hand. "I'm Charlie Foster."

"Sam McCall." Sam took an immediate dislike to the well-dressed, spiffed-up city slicker, but he couldn't have explained why. Still, Sam shook the man's hand. "This is my daughter, Lacey."

"Hey, sugar!" Charlie bent at the waist and gave her a toothy grin. "Aren't you a cutie?"

Lacey inched her way toward Sam and wrapped an arm around his leg. He put a comforting hand on her shoulder.

"Live around here?" Charlie asked.

"Not far." Sam crossed his arms over his chest.

"Toward the ski slopes or cattle country?"

"Don't know how to ski," Sam answered gruffly, deciding he didn't like the way he'd planted a kiss on Joy's cheek.

It was a stupid reaction.

It was dangerous.

But it was honest. And it irritated Sam like a cowboy's spurs raking against a rank bull's hide.

"Too bad. But you'll have to learn. Your little one will want to hit the slopes in a few years." Charlie leaned against the counter, crossing his arms like the resident expert. "This is a tight-knit community. Everybody knows everybody. And everybody else's business. Can't keep a secret in this town for long. We all watch out for one another, keep an eye on one another. Protect our own. Like Joy here."

"Charlie." A warning note entered her voice.

"Now, especially in her condition, we're all sort of protective of her. Why, Joy hadn't dated anyone for years. Turned me down a time or two. Imagine our surprise when she goes on vacation and meets some cowboy—"

"Charlie!"

He shrugged. "Oh, it don't matter to us, Joy. We love you. And want to take care of you, is all." Charlie looked to Sam again. "All the women in town are mothering her. And all the men are trying to marry her." He gave Joy a wink. "Isn't that right, love?"

A silence as loud as a clanging cymbal filled the store with a deafening crescendo. Joy turned as pale as the fluffy white flakes of snow falling outside the window. Sam stared at her hard, trying to see if she had a rounded belly or if he'd misunderstood the stranger's words. But the damn counter stood in his line of sight.

Slowly her gaze met his, her eyes dark and troubled as a storm descending on top of a mountain peak. She gave a silly, inappropriate laugh as her hand settled against her abdomen. ''Funny thing happened on my way home from Denver last April.''

Chapter Three

All I want for Christmas, Sam thought, is my sanity back. Somewhere along the road from his ranch to Jingle's city limits, he'd lost it. Really lost it. Was Joy standing here telling him she was pregnant? Insinuating it was *his* baby!

"You're pregnant?" His voice cracked. He took a step forward and stared at her oversize sweater. Her apprehensive gaze made him stop and want to race out the door.

"Very." She smoothed a hand down her belly, outlining the slight bulge, in a protective gesture. "Worked better than padding yesterday."

Sam's lungs stiffened, unable to suck in a breath. Sweat saturated his skin, as if he'd just broken a fever. He thought he'd been surprised when he'd stumbled inside her store yesterday and discovered underneath that Santa getup was his long-lost lover. Now he learned she was pregnant!

"Uh, I just dropped in to see if I could take you to supper." Charlie looked from Joy to Sam and back again. "Would you like to go to the tree lighting together?"

"Thanks, Charlie, but I need to work." Her blue eyes filled with an emotion Sam couldn't decipher. Nor did he want to. He wanted to run for the hills.

"Pop's feeling better and plans to make his appearance as you-know-who tonight." Her gaze flicked toward Lacey then slanted back toward Sam. "I need to help him get ready."

Sam's heartbeat became a faint flutter. Maybe it was the shock. Or fear. Or the thin air in this high elevation. He stared at the smooth round bundle hidden beneath Joy's colorful sweater.

It was a baby. All baby. Maybe *his* baby!

No, no, no! It couldn't be. Not *his*! They'd taken precautions. It didn't just happen that easily. Did it?

"Are you sure?" Charlie asked. "I could stick around and help you out."

"I'll be fine." Joy sounded firm and convincing.

Charlie backed toward the door. "Nice to meet you, Sam. I expect I'll see you around. Joy, if you need anything, I'm a phone call away."

As the door banged shut, a sudden sharp silence sliced the tension. Questions whipped through Sam's mind. Seconds whizzed by like bullets. "Was this what you meant when you said you were going through a lot? I mean, what trouble you mentioned you were having when we met?"

She shook her head. "I wasn't pregnant when I met you."

An ice cube of dread slid down his spine. "When are you due?"

Before she answered, he started calculating backward. How long had it been since that night in Denver? Was it possible? Good God, what if he was the father?

Joy picked at a knothole along the counter. "January."

He swallowed hard, forcing down a big ball of panic. He didn't know it was his. Or did he?

They'd used protection. Hadn't they? His brain scrambled, trying to recall the unimportant...now vital details of that night. The first time had been fast...too fast. But the next time had been slower, more tender, and he'd remembered to use protection. Had it only taken that first heated time? Damn. He'd never been so out of control. He'd forgotten they hadn't used anything. But the memory of Joy's sweetness, her passion, her absence the next morning had not been forgotten. If it wasn't his baby, then who else's could it be? Charlie's?

Sam's heart kicked into overdrive, pumping cold reality through his body. From the serious look in her eyes, he knew. Without a doubt. If she was pregnant, which she certainly appeared to be, then *he* was the baby's father.

Blood drained out of his head. He needed to sit down. He had to think. He had to figure this out.

"Daddy!" Lacey's frustrated whine penetrated the fog clouding his brain. She peered up at him, tugging on his jeans.

Slowly, his attention shifted. Lacey! His body jerked into a rigid stance. His daughter was hearing all of this! What the hell had he done?

The never-ending questions and distressing answers made his head spin. Getting a woman pregnant at the ripe old age of thirty-five was embarrassing, humiliating, horrifying enough without being caught in front of his five-year-old daughter.

He shoved his fingers through his hair. What had happened to his plans? This holiday was for Lacey! Now he might be planning it for another daughter or son. His legs felt loose and wobbly. He grabbed the counter beside him.

"Daddy, what's wrong? Are you okay?"

"Sam?" Joy reached for him.

He blinked and looked at his daughter again, really looked at her gold-flecked green eyes, freckled nose and curly hair. His daughter. His Lacey. Would she look at him differently someday when she understood all of this? Would she be hurt, feel betrayed? How would he explain?

"I'm okay, darlin'." *I only feel like I've been stomped on by a cantankerous old bull*. He tried to give her a smile, but it felt more like a contorted grimace.

"Lacey," Joy said in a tone that belied the tension sparking in the room, "why don't you look at some of the stuffed animals that arrived this morning. There's a cute little penguin at the back of the store that I bet you'd love."

"Okay." She skipped toward the bin but paused halfway down the first aisle. "Coming, Daddy?"

"Be there in a minute." Right after he got to the bottom of *this!*

Sam took the reprieve and worked on making his lungs operate. Each labored breath whistled in and out as if he were hyperventilating. He leaned heavily against the checkout counter. His shoulders started to feel the growing weight of added responsibilities as they settled firmly in place. He thought of stacks of medical bills, a sink full of bottles, sacks of formula, diapers, baby clothes…college! Tension tightened the muscles along his neck. His hands closed into fists as he tried to grasp reality. Now what? What would Joy expect from him?

Frankly, she seemed too calm with all of this. She looked cool and collected as she closed the register's drawer. Of course, she'd had time to absorb the shock, to prepare and plan. He'd been zapped out of the clear blue sky. Was she delighted to unload some of the burden onto him? Did she expect him to pay a hefty sum of child support?

Suddenly another question arose. Anger shot through him. If he hadn't wandered into Joy's store, if he hadn't run into her again, would she have *ever* told him about his baby? His stomach knotted. His short-clipped nails dug into his palms.

He glared at her as she put away receipts. Her motions were brusque, but he detected a slight tremor in her hand and felt the same spasm in his bones. A loud silence descended on the store. Sam struggled with where to begin, with what to say. Which question, in his long list of questions, should he ask first?

"Sorry about that." Joy kept her back to him. "Charlie's made himself my protector."

"Is he the father?"

Her head jerked up and she shot him a steely glance. "No." Her gaze softened on Sam. "This is pretty awkward, isn't it?"

"Do you get many ex-lovers coming through here?" Immediately, at the pain clouding her eyes, he regretted his words. Hell, she'd had more time to get used to this. What was he supposed to do or say?

"Need a drink?" She walked around the end of the counter.

His gaze shifted again to her belly, and his brain felt like a pillow stuffed with cotton. "A bottle."

"I know what you mean." Laughter made her voice even huskier, even sexier. "I had a hard time believing it myself when I first figured out why I was throwing up every day." She fanned herself with a flyer advertising the town's Christmas tree lighting set for tonight. "Is it warm in here?"

He shook his head. His bones ached with cold awareness.

"At least winter doesn't bother me this year. I could stand outside naked and not freeze these days." That planted an interesting picture in his mind. One he didn't need distracting him. "Something about being pregnant," she added, "makes you hot all the time."

Her words sparked a flame of heat inside him. Isn't that what had gotten him in this predicament in the first place? He jerked his thoughts away from that dangerous territory to focus on the issue at hand. "When did you learn you were...uh...pregnant?"

She sat on the edge of a stool and watched him closely for a moment before answering. She combed her fingers through her unruly curls. He remembered the soft, sweet fragrance of her hair, the silky threads teasing his skin, but shrugged aside the memory. That wasn't important now.

"Memorial Day," she answered. "I'd been sick

for about two weeks. Just couldn't keep anything down. I thought I had the flu or something. I kept going and going until I fainted outside the post office. Well, then my dad made me go see ol' Doc Benton. He ran a few tests and…bingo!''

"And you knew the father—"

Her icy gaze froze the rest of his comment in his throat. Why had he even started that question? He knew the answer. He'd known the truth the moment he'd learned she was pregnant.

"Yes," she said, her tone as frosty as her eyes. "*You* were the only one it could have been. I thought you understood that I'm not the type to sleep around. That night was… I was—"

A red blush brightened her cheeks, and he felt the heated blaze of it in the pit of his stomach. He staggered beneath the weight of the truth. "You've pulled the rug right out from under me."

"I suppose I did." She chuckled. Walking toward a side table, she poured two cups of red punch. "This is the strongest thing I have. Think of it as a sugar shot."

He downed it in one gulp and wished it had been a hundred proof. The sweetness made his insides constrict. When he swallowed to clear the cherry coating out of his throat, he looked deep into her eyes, searching for the answer to his next question. "And you decided to keep the baby?"

"Of course." She covered her stomach with her hands.

Stupid question, you jerk! He cursed himself. Why had he asked that? Was it a natural question?

Or fear resurfacing? After all, his ex-wife hadn't wanted Lacey.

"It never occurred to me not to." Her chin jutted out in a stubborn manner. "I want this baby. More than anything."

Her words struck him with the force of an avalanche. In spite of the circumstances, the inconvenience, the problems it would cause with his current situation, he knew at that moment he wanted this baby, too. He didn't know what he'd do with a baby, but he wanted to be a part of this little life, help it form and grow, witness all the things he'd missed during the first five years of Lacey's life. It was like starting with a clean slate. This was his second and possibly his last chance at fatherhood.

"Did it ever occur to you to contact m-m—" His gaze sought out Lacey who was playing with a bin full of stuffed animals. When he was satisfied his daughter wasn't paying attention he continued. "The father?"

She narrowed her gaze on him. "Yes."

He held his breath, waiting, wondering, cursing fate. "But?"

"You had enough obligations and commitments. You were overworked, overstressed, overwhelmed." She shrugged as if the decision had been simple. But he could read the tension tightening her features and understood the strain she'd experienced. She'd only seen a glimpse of him seven months ago. She hadn't known him any more than he'd known her.

Her hand settled on her belly, massaging the side gently. He imagined his baby growing inside her, and his stomach flopped on its side, like a fish out of water.

"I didn't know how to get in touch with you."

"If you'd stuck around for five minutes the morning after, maybe you would have learned."

She ignored his comment. "Or how you would handle it. I thought about telling you when you walked into my shop yesterday. But the timing wasn't right. I couldn't say in front of a roomful of kids, 'Hi, Sam, remember me? Good to see you. Oh, and by the way…!'"

He nodded, admitting it wouldn't have worked well. At least now he knew his reasoning skills were kicking back into gear.

"Then," she said with a heavy sigh, "yesterday you told me very clearly that you didn't have time for me, didn't want me in your life. Like I'd charged in and begged to be a part of your family. I figured you'd feel the same way about a baby, too. Maybe more so. So I decided not to tell you."

"Okay, I jumped the gun. But I was stunned. I wasn't expecting to see you. Or this. I was at a disadvantage. You knew the situation more clearly—" his gaze dropped to her belly "—much more so than I did. How could I have known?"

"You couldn't have. But an extra few hours didn't give me much time for clarity on the situation. I was confused, too, Sam. You can't blame me for protecting my baby—"

"Our—" he lowered his voice "—baby."

Something glimmered in her eyes, darkened them to a deep pool of emotion. He didn't know if he'd hurt her, made her boiling mad or somehow touched her. Frankly, he realized he didn't know Joy very well. But he'd have to get to know her. And fast.

Frustration unraveled his taut nerves. He started to pace, back and forth along the front counter. His world started to cave in on him.

"Look, Joy, this baby of ours—" He shook his head at the crazy twists of fate. They'd never even been a real couple, but now she carried his child. That gave them a bond that could never be severed.

Confused by the unfamiliar longings springing up inside him, he shoved his hand through his hair and diverted his attention away from her round belly. He let his gaze follow the strings of red, green and blue lights that decorated the store.

"Sam," Joy said, her tone low and confidential, "this isn't your problem. I can take care of myself and the baby. I've got it all planned. I don't need any help."

A cold sweat popped out along his forehead. Was she giving him the heave-ho? As his ex-wife had? Was she going to keep him from his baby? Not if he could help it.

"When I considered telling you about the baby," she said, "it was because I thought you had the right to know. But the baby, *my* baby has rights, too."

The hairs along the back of his neck stood at attention. "What do you mean?"

"I mean, you've got all you can handle with Lacey." She hesitated, drawing her full bottom lip between her teeth.

"Go on." He clenched his back teeth.

"I don't want a forced family." A sigh escaped

her parted lips like a puff of smoke. "I'm not convinced you're a good enough father."

A direct slap to his face couldn't have stung as much. It ripped through his pride, punched out his defenses and knocked him to his emotional knees. He staggered but bounced back, ready to defend himself. Dammit, he was trying to be the best father he could be! Didn't that count for something? "I was good enough for you to go to bed with."

Joy sucked in a breath. Her eyes turned as hard as glass. "Don't cast stones at me. You were there, too."

"I'm not judging. I'm saying I was good enough as a sperm donor." With his mind reeling from Joy's blunt words, he felt his heart pounding, the blood roaring in his ears, blocking out all reason. "How do you know I won't be a good father with this child?"

Frowning, she swiveled her stool to face him fully. She laid a hand on his arm. Unprepared for the gentleness of her touch, he tensed. "I'm sorry, Sam, I didn't mean to attack you. I don't want to hurt you. But you've got to know, I've really struggled with this. This hasn't been an easy decision for me, either. I tried to weigh the difference. Would a not-so-good father be better than no father at all?"

More frigid than an arctic blast, a chill swept through him. He could only blame himself. Not only had he screwed up as a father with Lacey, but he might have destroyed his chance to be a father to this baby…before it was even born.

"Maybe," she said, "you should concentrate on

Lacey right now. We don't have to decide anything today. We can figure this out later.''

''What about you?''

Her eyes softened, the color deepening to the hue of the distant mountains. ''I'll be okay.'' She ducked her chin and lovingly patted her rounded stomach. ''We'll be fine.''

She was cutting him loose! He couldn't believe it. She wasn't demanding money or compensation or help. She wasn't pleading for him to marry her. She was releasing him from his obligations. At the same time, she'd sliced away a piece of his heart.

For a moment, he floundered, trying to think of a comeback, trying to decide what to do. Part of him wanted to gather up Lacey and whisk her away before the consequences crushed their struggling family. But he'd never run away from anything in his life. And he wasn't about to start now.

His determination gaining ground, he faced Joy again, feeling stronger, more decisive, ready to handle the situation. ''So, what we shared meant nothing to you?''

''More than it should have.'' She met his gaze with a bold, direct challenge of her own.

''What will you do?'' he asked, his voice roughened with a helpless futility. ''How will you manage without my help?''

''Many women survive without an almighty male.''

''I'm not being chauvinistic. I'm being practical, dammit.''

She sighed. ''I'm staying here. This is my life…my home. Pop's here. He'll help for a while.

The baby and I will be okay. We have a place to live. I have a job. And someday, when Pop decides to retire, I'll own the shop. It's not a glamorous life but it's comfortable. It's safe. It's home. And it's a darn good place to raise a child.''

He couldn't argue with her. Problem was—where did he fit into this scenario? ''You have good medical care? A close hospital?''

''Yes, of course. You don't need to worry about that.''

Her resistance to his concern irritated him. ''It's my job to worry. I'm the father.''

''The biological one.''

Her words sliced through him, pained him more than he could have ever imagined. He stared at her belly, wondering about the child inside. Was it a boy? A girl? What would its name be? Would it have dark hair, like his? Or red, like Joy's? Blue eyes or gray? And what of its future?

Before he could think better of his actions, he reached toward her. His hand trembled, the nerves in his fingers contracting. He prayed she wouldn't move away. As his ex-wife had. She'd hated being pregnant, resented him for making her that way. When he'd tried to touch her, feel their baby moving and squirming inside her, she'd pushed him away.

Wary of Joy's response now, he slowly, tenderly, reverently touched the rounded side of her stomach. He felt her quick intake of breath. But she held still. Their eyes met, as if the intimacy they'd shared that one night replayed in both of their minds, pulling them together and pushing them apart simultaneously. His pulse thundered in his ears.

He laid his palm against the roundness. It felt unnatural, like a basketball, taut and hard. He remembered sliding his hand down the flat plane of her stomach when they'd made love. Her flesh had been sensitive, responsive, ticklish. Now, as slow as the first spring thaw, he smoothed his hand along the side and over the middle. A trembling started deep inside him.

Then her stomach jerked. He yanked his hand away as if he'd felt a jolt of electricity.

"It's okay." She offered him a tender smile. Her voice floated as soft as a snowflake. Taking his hand between hers, she placed it back on her stomach.

Her gentle touch, the soft glow in her eyes and the warmth of her skin beneath the sweater made his heart stop. When he felt a movement, like a butterfly's wing, beneath his palm, his heart lurched.

"It's the baby moving. Can you feel her?"

He nodded, words jamming up in his throat. His heart swelled with powerful emotions that he couldn't decipher.

"She's pretty active this time of day. But at night, well, she's a real night owl."

A lump formed in his throat and tightened his chest. "She?"

The corners of her eyes crinkled with a gentle smile. "I had an ultrasound a couple of weeks ago. Everything was fine." She must have read his questioning gaze correctly. She settled a comforting hand on his arm. But it didn't soothe him. She stirred something inside him, something raw and unpredictable, something electrifying. "I decided I'd had enough surprises with this pregnancy. So when they asked if I wanted to know the baby's sex, I said yes.''

Jerking his thoughts back to the baby moving beneath his hand, his voice quavered when he asked, ''And it's a girl?''

She nodded. Tears welled in her eyes, but she blinked them away. ''At least they said they were fairly sure. They always leave room for a margin of error.''

Sam placed both hands on his baby, feeling it move and jostle around inside Joy's body. His throat contracted, shutting off all possible words. His thoughts whirled around his brain, unable to land on a single cohesive response. He remained perfectly still, feeling the subtle movements of the baby beneath his palm, touching the warmth of Joy's taut stomach, experiencing this Christmas miracle.

A peace settled over him. Once again, he felt connected to Joy, the way it had been when they'd first met, when they'd made love. Back then, pain had drawn them to each other. Now their baby brought them together. Maybe the miracle he'd prayed for hadn't come in the package he'd anticipated. But it was here, nevertheless. His chest swelled with hope and promise and sudden overwhelming love for this unborn child. *His child.*

Joy felt her knees tremble, and her guard started to slip. She'd promised herself not to react to Sam as a man. But he touched her stomach so reverently. Were those tears shimmering in his eyes? She stood so close to him that his breath became hers. She absorbed his warm, masculine scent of spicy cologne and tangy soap. Memories flooded her mind with hot kisses and bold caresses.

As he stared at her stomach as if he could see the baby moving inside her, she was reminded of the intimacy they'd shared. She watched his throat contract, the skin stretching over his Adam's apple each time it dipped and sprang back into place. A warm, sated glow flowed through her. No matter his angry words, his shock, he was moved by what they'd created out of their individual, maybe selfish needs.

He cared.

A part of her had needed to know that, needed to feel for one more minute the way they'd felt together that night they'd made love. Now all of her doubts evaporated. She hadn't imagined what they'd shared. She hadn't conjured it up out of thin air or from some panicked need inside her. More than just their bodies had joined. A part of their souls had touched as well and would live on in this child.

Pushing back the impulse to lay her hand over his, to touch him, to strengthen the connection between them, she resisted. Her muscles ached with the effort. She had to think of her baby first. She had to make decisions for her daughter. She moved away, breaking the contact with him, as if severing an umbilical cord.

When he looked up at her with those warm gray eyes, she felt her resolve melt a degree, despite her determination. He placed his hand along the side of her jaw, his thumb rubbing her skin and making delicious sensations shimmy down her spine. She didn't know she could feel these things as pregnant as she was.

She wanted to lean into his warmth, feel his mouth cover hers, taste his need once more. A part of her wanted his arms to come around her and hold her and chase away her fears. But she resisted. She'd made this decision on her own. And she'd stand on her own two feet.

"I'm going to be a part of our child's life," he said with solid conviction.

Needing her space, her freedom, she took a step away from him. Then she stared at him with disbelief. "This is *my* child." She wrapped her arms around her belly. "You can visit. But this is my child. I'm going to raise her. Alone."

"I want...need to be a part of her life. I don't want to be some guy that drifts in and out of her life periodically. Not like I was with Lacey."

"How do you expect to do that? You think a weekend daddy is the answer? What about Lacey? She needs you, too."

"I am thinking about Lacey." His jaw hardened. "About both of my daughters."

Joy felt a lump form in her throat as he declared that this child she was carrying was his.

"This baby needs me, too. I may have failed Lacey before now, but I'm going to change that. I'm not going to fail this baby."

"You can't use my child to redeem yourself."

"It's my child, too."

She shivered with cold apprehension. "This is ridiculous."

"No, it's not." He put a hand on her shoulder when she turned away. He forced her to face him. Leaning down, he stared into her eyes. His determined gaze looked like solid steel and made her knees weak. "There's a simple solution."

"What?" She lifted her chin defiantly.

"We have to get married," he said, his voice low and husky, warm and gentle, firm and uncompromising. His hand touched her stomach again, connecting them once more in a common bond.

The familiarity and intimacy of the gesture combined was an assault on her senses. Joy's mind reeled. Her ears filled with the sound of pumping blood. "What?"

His gaze softened, and he touched the corner of her mouth with his thumb. "Marry me."

Chapter Four

In less time than it took to blink, Joy had the answer to Sam's less-than-romantic proposal.

"No." She crossed her arms over the top of her rounded belly. She wanted love, a marriage grounded in devotion. Sam wasn't offering anything remotely close to that. He didn't even want her. Only her baby. How could she agree to marry him? "Absolutely not."

A tick started in his temple. "Joy—"

"Hear me out." She took a step away from him. His mere touch shattered her nerves and made her vulnerable, and she couldn't afford irrational hormonal reactions now. She had to be strong. No matter what she had once felt for Sam, even if it had been irrational, crazy and dangerous, she couldn't rely on emotions, biological urges or the seductive need to feel his strong arms around her, soothing her fears, promising security. "Just because we shared one night—"

"One passionate night." With a searing look he stirred up too many sizzling memories for her to ignore.

Her body tingled with awareness. She remembered how his exploring hands had aroused desires she'd never experienced. She remembered how his hot kisses made her desperate for more. And she remembered lying curled against his side, feeling safe and cherished…until the glaring light of morning shattered her dream.

"We shared one night," she repeated firmly, not giving into the memories. "Passionate or not, it is not a foundation for marriage. A lifelong commitment. If and when I marry it will be for love. And only love. I will not marry for convenience or convention's sake."

She took a deep, steadying breath. "You have no obligations here, Sam. I'm not holding you accountable for—" she shifted her gaze to the back of the store where Sam's daughter still played quietly with the stuffed animals "—for anything."

"I am. I'm responsible."

"It took two to…well, you know." Her skin ignited, burned with awareness, embarrassment, humiliation. "I'm accountable, too. And I can handle this. It's not your fault. It simply happened. And I'll deal with the consequences. Alone."

"You don't understand." His voice was filled with conviction. "I'm holding you accountable, too. You should be willing to do the right thing. Not for you. For our child."

She bristled. "I am! Good grief. I'm going to provide her with a home and all the love she can stand."

"But at the same time you're willing to deprive her of a real family? Of her own daddy? Of knowing her half sister?'' His voice grew louder, demanding, insisting she was wrong. He shoved his fingers through his hair and blew a puff of air toward his forehead, as if trying to contain his turbulent emotions.

If nothing else, Joy realized, Sam had a broad streak of honor running through him. How many men would have taken this opportunity to run, to leave their responsibilities far behind? She reluctantly—if not grudgingly—respected him for his stance, but it didn't mean they were compatible. Honor be damned. It sure didn't mean they should commit to a lifetime of misery. That wouldn't be good for Lacey or her baby.

It was more complicated than Sam's sense of honor and responsibility. She remembered when she'd first met him, how he'd spoken of his daughter, how he'd regretted having missed so much of her young life, how he'd been racked with guilt. Now he simply wanted repentance through this baby for what he hadn't been able to give Lacey. It had nothing to do with wanting or loving the baby. Or her.

''Sam...'' Her voice softened with understanding but remained firm with her own convictions. ''I appreciate your reasons. I even respect you for wanting to do, as you said, 'right' by this baby. But a marriage is more than creating a family. It's a lifetime commitment. It's a precious decision that shouldn't be taken lightly.''

''I'm not. I'm serious about marrying you.''

''It can't work.''

"Why?" Was that genuine pain gleaming in his eyes?

"Because you..." *You don't love me.*

She swallowed the unreasonable hurt she felt at that thought. It made no sense. She didn't love him, either. But she'd felt so close to him that one night. So close. And now so far apart.

"Because," she finally managed to say, "we don't love each other."

"How do we know? We haven't given love time. You ran out on me before—"

"Sam, you don't know that we would have fallen in love then. It was a crazy thing we did. But it would be even crazier if we were to get married now. You can't force love. It happens or it doesn't. Besides, if we were to get married and it didn't work out...if we ended up getting divorced, then that could cause more damage.

"So, don't worry about us." She placed her hand protectively over her stomach and felt her baby move in response. "I'm capable of taking care of myself and my baby."

"Our baby." He ground his teeth together.

She sensed his determination, recoiled from it. "Sam, I am not going to marry you. Not now. Not ever. You can visit the baby. I understand this child is part of you, too. I won't deprive her of knowing her father. But we won't be a traditional family."

"You don't know what you're saying."

"Yes, I do." She met his challenging gaze, squared her jaw to match his and stood toe to toe with him. She would not back down. "You were right. I've had more time to think about this. You're making a rash decision. One we'd both regret. Give it some time, and you'll see I'm right.''

"About what?'' A familiar voice broke through the tension crackling between them.

Joy turned toward her father, who'd descended the back staircase as quietly as a mouse. Or had she been too intent on Sam to hear his approach? Her father walked toward the checkout counter, his worn boots scuffing the hardwood floor she'd swept earlier. His blue eyes looked clearer than when she'd fixed him breakfast, but his nose still looked red from the cold he'd been fighting.

Concern outweighed the anger and frustration she felt toward Sam. "Hi, Pop. How are you feeling?''

"I've had about all the rest I can stand.'' He gave a gurgly cough. "If I watch any more of them golderned soap operas I'm going to be hooked and have to retire.''

She smiled. Her father wasn't the type to lounge around letting time get away from him. "Did you need me to get you anything?''

"Not a thing. I'm not used to being waited on.''

When his attention shifted to Sam, she swallowed hard. She hadn't told Pop about Sam. Oh, she'd told him she'd made a mistake and gotten pregnant. Her father had been understanding, sympathetic, supportive. He'd respected her privacy, never once asking who the father was. But he didn't know the cowboy had shown up in Jingle.

"Hello, young fellow.'' Pop held out his hand to Sam. "I'm Joy's father. Earl Chase. Are you new in town? I don't remember seeing you before.''

"Um, Pop,'' Joy started to say, scrambling for

words to explain this new predicament, for a way to convey to Sam to keep quiet. She didn't want her father upset anymore by her foolish mistakes.

Sam read Joy's hesitation. Or was it panic? He wiped the sweat off his palm and shook the older gentleman's hand, clasping it firmly, respectfully. Despite Earl's rounded belly, there was nothing soft about his handshake. Or the keen, sharp look in his blue eyes.

As with everything else in his life, Sam took the bull by the horns. If her father wanted to punch him in the nose for getting his daughter in this predicament, he'd face his punishment like a man. His own jaw hardened at the thought of some jerk getting Lacey pregnant someday in the distant future. If that happened, he'd hunt the man down and... "Sir, I want—"

"Pop," Joy interrupted. Her eyes narrowed as if trying to communicate something to him. But what?

Did she know how her father would react meeting the man who'd gotten his daughter pregnant? He wouldn't hide behind Joy. "Sir, I'm Sam McCall."

"Proud to know you." Earl didn't seem to recognize Sam's name. Hadn't Joy told him?

Perplexed, he glanced back at Joy. Her eyes darted between him and her father. She looked anxious, as if she didn't want to discuss their situation, as if she wanted to sweep it under the rug. But she couldn't, no more than she could hide her growing abdomen. Surely, her father knew she was pregnant. Hadn't that lanky man who'd proposed to her earlier said the whole town knew she was expecting? Sam wasn't about to run from his responsibility, and he wanted Joy's father to know his intentions.

Earl tugged on his short-cropped snowy white beard. The burly gentleman looked as friendly as Kris Kringle even though he was dressed like a lumberjack in his bright red plaid shirt, dark blue jeans and cowboy boots. "Whatever you're trying to change my daughter's mind about, young man, you better know right off that she's a might stubborn. Gets that from her mama. Once she sets her mind to something, there's no going back."

"That so?" A wry smile tugged at Sam's mouth. He'd started to learn firsthand how bullheaded Joy could be. "So you're saying it's a lost cause to try?" Not that he'd stop.

"Nope. Just saying you're gonna have to prove your point to her. Then give her plenty of room to make up her own mind. Let her think it was her idea. And even that's no guarantee."

Let her think it was her idea to get married? How the heck would he accomplish that? "I'll keep that in mind. But you might warn your daughter that I've got a stubborn streak all my own."

The older gentleman's eyes twinkled like Christmas lights. He chuckled deeply, making his round belly shake. "Maybe she's found her match then."

"Pop—" Joy stepped forward, anxiety lining her forehead.

But Sam had something he had to say first. "Mr. Chase—"

"Call me Earl." Then he glanced around the store. With a sly grin, he added, "Or Santa when any kids are around."

How could he tell this kind old soul, this man who personified Santa Claus, that he'd gotten his daughter pregnant? He swallowed a ball of regret. "I want you to know, sir, that I plan on doing right by your daughter."

"Oh?"

"Sam—" Joy injected. "I really think you should, um, come back later when I have time to help you with your Christmas decorations. Pop's obviously tired and…"

He ignored her panicked expression and kept his gaze trained on her father. "I've already offered to marry Joy. Now I just have to convince her. I could use your help."

Earl crossed his arms over his chest. "I see. And Joy said no, eh?"

"Yes, sir. But I truly think it's for the best…for the baby…that we get married. Don't you?"

"Sam," Joy stated emphatically, "you've gone too far. I will not let you bully me into matrimony."

"You heard my daughter, young man. She doesn't want to get married."

"But certainly you believe it would be better—"

"Are you the baby's father?" he asked point-blank.

"Yes, sir."

Earl looked at his daughter, who gave a succinct nod. He took a full minute to absorb the impact of that revelation. Then he shifted his attention back to Sam and crossed his arms over his broad chest. "Have you ever been married, young man?"

"Yes, sir."

"And divorced, I assume."

Sam almost wished the older gentleman would punch him out rather than strike at him with these questions. "Yes, sir."

"And was your marriage worth it?"

His gaze shifted toward Lacey, who was making a stuffed penguin talk to a fluffy white seal. "Yes, sir. It gave me my daughter, Lacey, over there."

Earl's gaze followed and softened as he looked at Sam's daughter playing. "But did the marriage and divorce benefit your child?"

"I don't know." He didn't know much of anything these days. "But I do think she's better off with me than living with her mother."

"Well, young man, I don't know about that. But I do know my daughter." He placed an arm around Joy, pulling her close to his bulky side, forming a barrier against him. "You're a father already, so you know the love a father has for his child. Can't be severed. I bet you'd do anything for your daughter. Right?"

"Yes, sir."

"So would I." He gave his daughter a gentle squeeze. "She'll make a fine mother. But I don't know what kind of a father or husband you'd make. So, I'll have to side with her for the time being."

"Fine." Sam felt his shoulders tense with frustration. "I'll prove my case to both of you."

"DADDY!" LACEY TOOK that awkward moment to skip over to them. "Aren't we gonna get some stuff to decorate our tree?"

"You bet, darlin'." He ruffled her hair and tucked her against his side, mirroring Earl and Joy. He'd stated his case and now he felt as if he were fighting for the very existence of his family.

"Is Joy going to help?" Lacey's gaze lifted to the woman who'd thrown a wrench into his life, then widened when she noticed the big, burly bearded man. She started tugging on Sam's jeans, but he was intent on Joy's response.

"Well, Lacey..." Joy started to say, her voice hesitant as if she was on the verge of backing out of their original deal.

"Of course she's going to help. She promised." Sam met her defiant gaze with his own brand of stubbornness. "Didn't you?"

"Yes, I promised." Her mouth thinned into a straight line, and Sam smiled. He clearly remembered how buttery soft her mouth could be, melting his resolve, stirring up a fire inside him.

"Aren't you going to take us to find a real tree tomorrow?" Sam pressed.

"If Pop's feeling well enough for me to leave him with the store, otherwise—"

"Now, don't you worry about me. You go and have a good time," Earl said, rubbing his hand along his beard as if to hide a smirk. Was the old gentleman on Sam's side after all?

"Are you the real Santa?" Lacey asked, staring up at Earl with a slack jaw.

Earl patted his belly and chuckled. "Hello, cutie pie. You must be Lacey."

Her eyes rounded. "You know my name."

"Sure I do."

Lacey grabbed Sam's hand. "Daddy! He knowed my name. How'd he do that?"

"I don't know, darlin'." He tried to think back. Had he used his daughter's name earlier? He couldn't remember. But he wasn't about to dim the light shining in her eyes. He didn't know if miracles existed or not, but this town had already had a magical effect on Lacey. And if Christmas wishes came true, then he'd be sure to make his wish tonight, standing next to Joy, with his daughter by his side.

"Where's your red suit?" Lacey asked, studying Joy's father closely.

"At the cleaners," Earl answered. "I can't wear it every day."

Lacey nodded thoughtfully. "Where's Rudolph and the other reindeer? Do you keep them out back?"

"Nope. They're at the North Pole." He gave Lacey a wink. "It's too warm down here for them."

She giggled in response. "But what about the elves...and Mrs. Santa...and...?"

"Lacey," Sam said, interrupting his daughter's string of questions. "Give Santa a break. He's been sick."

Suddenly his daughter's forehead crumpled. "Are you gonna be okay?"

"Right as rain." His smile made his cheeks rounder and rosier.

"Is your beard real?"

"Lacey..."

Earl leaned forward. "Give it a tug and see for yourself."

She did and her mouth popped open. Then she looked at Santa's rounded tummy. Taking a hesitant step forward she poked it with her finger as if he were the Pillsbury Doughboy.

Earl gave a hearty, robust laugh that sounded an awful lot like ''Ho, ho, ho.''

''He is,'' Lacey said, her voice full of awe. ''He is the real Santa. Joy told me you got sick. That's why she took your place in the parade. She said you were real. That you could make Christmas wishes come true.''

Earl knelt down beside Lacey, propping his elbow on his knee. ''I try my best, sugar. Are you going to come to the Christmas tree lighting in town tonight? That's the best place to make Christmas wishes.''

''Can we, Daddy? Can we?''

''Sure, darlin'. Why don't we come by the store and pick up some decorations, then take Joy with us to the square?''

''Sam—'' Joy's voice held a warning note ''—I don't think that's a good idea.''

''Why not?'' Lacey asked. ''Don't you like us?''

''Of course, but...''

''Then how come you won't come with us? Do you have to play Santa again?''

''Nope,'' Earl said, ''I'm lighting the Christmas tree tonight.''

''Then why?'' Lacey persisted, as only a five-year-old could. Sam had never thought he'd be so grateful for his daughter's continual questions. But he smiled down at her, admiring her persistence.

''All right,'' Joy said with a resigned sigh.

Sam gave a quick nod of victory. ''We'll pick you up here.''

JOY SETTLED THE RED VELVET cap on her father's head. He stared at her silently with the same weighted stare he'd been using all afternoon. Her nerves felt frayed. Ignoring his silent questions bombarding her, she adjusted his Santa belt then stepped away, pleased that he looked as robust as ever. But not jolly. Not with that serious frown on his face.

"Okay," she said with exasperation, "go ahead and say it."

He shook his head, making the furry ball at the end of his cap sway. "Nope. You're a grown woman. You know what you're doing."

Did she? Did she really? She definitely had her doubts.

"Look, Pop, you don't understand."

"And I don't need to." He ran his hands down the sloping curve of his rounded belly. Pop didn't need padding, either. "It's between you and that fellow…Sam."

Sam. Just his name stirred up a whirlwind of emotions.

"Fine then." She was more than eager to dismiss the whole discussion. "You're all ready for the ceremony tonight. How do you feel?"

"Fine."

"Feverish?"

"No."

"Headache still?"

"No."

"Want some more of your cold medicine?" She turned toward the back office where she had a good stock of aspirin and sinus medicines.

"I'm fine." He took her hand and pulled her

around to face him. "But I can see you're not. Want to tell your ol' pop about it?"

"There's nothing to tell."

He touched her rounded belly, which almost bumped into his. "I think there's a lot to tell. I've been patient with you, Joy."

"You've been wonderful, Pop." Tears of gratitude swelled in her eyes. "I wish I hadn't gotten myself in such a mess. I know I'm not the only one affected. I've disappointed you and I know you feel more of a burden now. But believe me, I'm going to take care of this baby. You won't have to lift a finger. I won't ask for any money or—"

"Joy, honey, you're my daughter. My life. I'd give my right arm for you, even my life. I don't care about the money. I simply care about you and what's best for you and this baby."

She pressed her lips together to keep from leaning on his shoulder once again and sobbing. What a mess she'd made of her life. No, she wouldn't think that. This, her baby, was her Christmas miracle. She needed this baby, probably as much, if not more so, than the baby needed her right now. The umbilical cord acted two ways—giving the baby sustenance while giving Joy hope and a future.

"I know you think I should give Sam a chance. After all, he's the baby's father. But you don't understand, Pop."

"I understand more than you think."

She tilted her head up to look at the kind sincerity in her father's dazzling blue eyes. "Thank you."

"Just remember what you told me, honey. You're not the only one affected by these circumstances.

And I'm not talking about me. I'm referring to that man you unceremoniously refused to marry this afternoon. And I'm also meaning that baby you're carrying. You can't be selfish now. Not when you're gonna be a mama.''

"Would you have me marry a man who doesn't love me?" she asked, her heart pounding with defiance.

"No." He cupped her chin as he had since she was a child. It was a comforting gesture, and her heart tightened with emotions. "But I'd also have you give him a chance."

A chance. Could she do that? Could she risk her heart on a slim if not impossible dream?

Chapter Five

It was anything but a silent night. Joy's heart beat louder than the brass band. Lacey held one of her gloved hands, and Sam stood so close she could catch whiffs of his cologne with almost every breath.

He unnerved her.

He irritated her. Who did he think he was? Demanding they get married!

He made her heart pound, her skin tighten with need and her body remember all they'd shared together.

Wrapping her arms across her middle, she nestled inside her wool coat, not so much against the chill of the winter night, but to protect her from Sam, at least his affect on her, and to keep herself from making another mistake with him.

She gazed at the podium, even though she was more aware of *him* than the program. Behind the dais, a dark green pine rose majestically like the mountains in the distance. The North Star winked and blinked in the night sky above as if it held the honored position on the top of the town's Christmas tree. She'd watched this traditional ceremony every year of her life. Seeing the tree now with the same decorations gave her a sense of continuity and hope. This is what she wanted for her own daughter. She wanted her child to grow up with the love and sense of community she'd been blessed with.

That thought made her wonder if Sam was right. Was she denying her daughter the family she herself had been given, then denied?

With a suppressed sigh, she realized things did change. She'd learned that lesson as a child on a cold night in February when her mother hadn't arrived home. The news of the car crash and her mother's death had wrecked Joy's life, turned her world upside down and shattered her childhood.

Joy had been raised on traditions, lived a traditional life, always tried to do the right thing. But then she'd met Sam. And once again, her world had changed. Forever.

It seemed like a another lifetime when a friend introduced her to Sam in Denver and she'd agreed to have dinner with the soft-spoken cowboy who tried to hide the pain in his eyes. She'd never connected with a man so quickly or so completely. Making love to him had been the most natural culmination of their time together. But it had also been an incredible mistake. Because she'd known instantly that she could love this cowboy with all her heart.

But that was the problem and what had propelled her from his bed. Knowing she could love him scared her, but not as much as knowing he wasn't the settling-down type. He was a rodeo cowboy, always on the road, always heading to another rodeo. She'd wondered if she'd been just another prize along the way. She'd fled his bedroom before he'd been able to scramble for an escape route the next morning.

Looking at him now, as he pointed out the band to his daughter, she realized she'd been wrong about him. At least partly. Maybe he was the settling-down type. After all, he'd given up the rodeo for his daughter. He was trying to make up for lost time with Lacey. And he wanted to marry Joy in order to form a family for their new baby.

But that wasn't enough. She wanted more.

And that's what broke her heart. He didn't want her. He wanted her baby. Their family. Not her. The pain resonated through her, vibrating in her heart, and she resolved not to let herself fall for him again. It would only lead to greater heartache.

A trumpet note, a lonesome, trailing sound, lifted toward the mountain peaks surrounding Jingle as the band started warming up their instruments and cold fingers. A winter freeze made the air snap like brittle tree limbs. Joy shivered inside her coat.

"Are you cold?" Sam's whisper caressed her ear and stirred up a raging fire inside her.

"I'm fine. Just fine." But was she? It had been easy to push aside the memories of Sam as she'd begun to anticipate having a baby. But with him standing next to her, looking at her with concern, she had a hard time shutting down the way her body responded to him and partitioning off her heart.

"We don't have to stay, if you're uncomfortable." Little puffs of breath drew her attention to his mouth, reminding her how sensuous and tender he could be. "Maybe you need to sit down. You've been on your feet all day. I could walk you back to your shop. Get you warmed up."

"No, no." No! She didn't want him warming her up! She didn't want his tender concern, either. "Lacey's looking forward to seeing Santa in all his regalia. She wants to make her Christmas wish."

"Me, too." His voice took on a seductive tone, dipping low and coiling her insides with an irrepressible heat. "What are you going to wish for, Joy?"

That he'd leave her alone. That he'd forget about his marriage proposal. That she could get back to her regular, normal life. But she was beginning to realize that was impossible. Her life had taken a definite detour. It would never be the same. And neither would she. Because she'd never be able to forget Sam.

"Want to know what I'm going to wish for?" His dark gaze moved over her face and settled on her mouth.

A hot flash surged inside and made her want to strip off her coat. But she resisted. It wasn't Sam. It was the baby. Hormones.

"No," she managed to say, determined not to learn about his wishes or fantasies. She had enough trouble ignoring her own.

He gave a wry smile. "Gives a wish more potency if you don't tell. So I'll keep it to myself."

And she'd keep hers hidden within her heart. It would be a battle of wills to see which would come true.

"ARE YOU READY?" Sam asked, hurrying Lacey into the Christmas shop and out of the cold wind the next morning.

Joy looked up from the box from which she was unloading seasonal cards with pictures of Santa and snowmen covering the front. She stood slowly, arching her back to accommodate her swollen abdomen. "Well, I don't know if I should leave or not."

Concern tightened Sam's gut, and he froze. Was she trying to back out now? Then he noticed the tension around her mouth. Fear slammed into him. "What do you mean? Are you…is everything okay? With you? The baby?"

She dismissed his questions with a shrug of her shoulder and gentle wave of her hand. "It's not me. I'm fine. It's Pop." She lowered her voice. "He coughed most of last night. He overdid it yesterday. And that cold air last night wasn't good for him. He needs to rest."

Frustrated that she was simply looking for an excuse to be rid of him, Sam closed the door with a bang, and the bell above him jingled. As much as he wanted to hold her to her promise, he also didn't want to come between her and her father, especially if Earl really was sick. "Does he need to go to the doctor?" Another plan formed in his mind. "We could help you take him to the clinic."

Lacey stamped the packed snow off her boots. "You mean we're not going to get our tree today?"

"Nonsense, cutie pie." Around the corner of an aisle, Earl marched like a man with a mission. "You're going to get your tree. And, Joy, I am not a child to be coddled. For Pete's sake, I've been handling this store for years. I can take care of it without your help for a day.''

''But, Pop—''

He propped his fists on his hips and arched his white eyebrows. ''Young lady, I've been listening to you harp about my health the past week. You're not going to ruin this day for Lacey because I have a persistent cough. Doc Benton said it would take a while for all this gunk to clear up. I'm fine.''

''Are you really sick?'' Lacey asked. ''Daddy says when I'm sick I gotta stay in bed and eat chicken noodle soup.''

''Well, I've been doing exactly that, sugar dumplin'. But I can't wallow around in bed forever. And a man's gotta have something more substantial to eat than soup. Besides, I just have a little sniffle. Now, don't you worry.'' He put a gentle hand on Lacey's shoulder. ''Nothin' for you…or anyone else—'' he shifted his gaze to Joy ''—to worry about.''

''I saw you last night,'' Lacey said, looking up at Santa, who wore a blue plaid flannel shirt and khakis instead of his red velvet garb.

''You did!'' He laughed and once again Sam heard a distinctive ''ho, ho, ho'' underlining the robust sound. ''What did you think of the tree lighting?''

''I liked it.''

''Did you sing along with the band?''

She nodded.

''Did you make your wish?''

''Yep,'' she answered.

''Yes, sir,'' Sam corrected her.

"Well, good. Now, you come by on Friday and sit on my lap. Because you've gotta tell Santa your wish, too. That's the rule."

She grinned. "Can I, Daddy?"

Sam gave a quick nod, still marveling at the recent changes in his daughter. Before he'd moved to Jingle, he'd been eager to make her smile. Now he just wanted to see her smile last. "You bet, darlin'."

"Now—" Santa patted Lacey on the back "—you three get out of here. Go find a tree and make this little girl's Christmas wish come true."

Joy's eyes softened as she looked at Lacey. "Well, if you're sure. But take it easy, Pop. If you start to feel feverish, just close the shop for the day and call Doc Benton. Or if you're feeling tired, then go lie down. Or if—"

"I know how to take care of myself. I'm the one who taught you self-reliance. Remember?" Earl shooed them toward the door, waving his arms as if he were herding cows. "Go on. Daylight's wastin'."

"Can we get you anything while we're out?" Sam asked, grateful the old man wasn't too sick to mind the store, and even more grateful for the opportunity to spend time with Joy...and his baby. Maybe he'd figure out a way to rope her into his family permanently.

Earl scratched his head. "Where you all going? To the Cannaday's?"

"I thought that would be the best place to start," Joy said as she grabbed her coat and hat behind the front counter. "Did you bring an ax?"

"What for?" Sam asked, moving forward to take her coat.

"Someone has to chop down the tree."

Earl chuckled. "Joy would, but I think she's a little too cumbersome these days."

"Or too hormonal to be trusted with a sharp object." Sam added with a friendly wink.

She scowled at him.

Sam held open her coat for her. "Let me help you."

She met his gaze, her blue eyes turning gray with defiance. "I can do it myself."

Sam heard the rebellion in her voice but couldn't take it too seriously, especially when he couldn't take his eyes off her pink mouth, the full bottom lip or the bowlike curve along the top. He remembered the velvety texture of her mouth against his. She had opened to him so willingly. But he knew she wouldn't again. Not now. Not with so much between them.

His gaze shifted to the blue sweater with white snowflakes covering her rounded stomach. He wanted to place his hand against her, feel the baby…his baby moving. His heart swelled with awe as he remembered that first touch, the first stirring of his baby. But it hadn't been just the baby that had knocked him for a loop.

Joy's warmth had reached out and pulled him in, tangling his insides into tedious knots. His gaze slid back up her now-voluptuous body, which he wanted to explore. He had a sudden urge to close the gap between them and steal a quick kiss. Or maybe a longer, more meaningful one. It was an absurd thought, one he quickly pushed away.

He gave her coat a shake, to emphasize he simply

wanted to help her, not take advantage of her. But he knew the truth. Ever since he'd seen her again, he hadn't been able to get her out of his mind. At night while lying in bed he remembered that night they'd shared. His body automatically overheated with the desire to repeat those rare, special moments.

She's pregnant! She didn't want romance. And neither did he. He simply wanted to marry her, to make their family complete. For the baby.

But his libido seemed to be getting in the way. Or it could if he acted on any of his recent impulses.

Looking at Joy, with a thick sweater covering her narrow shoulders, full breasts and rounded stomach, he couldn't help wanting more. Wanting her. Was that so wrong?

No. But he also wouldn't let that desire trip him up and ruin whatever chance he might have to marry her. He sensed her wariness. That night they'd made love, something had made her bolt. And he'd better find out what.

The standoff between them continued. Sam wasn't about to back down from his offer to help her on with her coat. Was she that determined to do everything by herself?

Her father gave a gruff chuckle and shook his head. "Don't castrate the man for trying to be a gentleman, Joy."

She glanced over her shoulder. "Pop—"

Sam took the opportunity to step closer. Immediately, she snapped her head in his direction. Only the coat prevented them from touching. If he'd dared, he could have dipped his head and taken her mouth in a demanding kiss. But the timing wasn't right. Soon, he thought, he'd have to see if his memory was as accurate about Joy as he imagined it to be.

"If it'll make you feel any better," he said, suppressing a chuckle, "I'll let you hold my coat for me later."

"Don't count on it." She frowned and shoved one arm into the wool sleeve.

Shifting slightly, she turned her back on Sam and worked her other hand and arm into the coat. Standing so close, he noticed an enticing auburn curl spiraling along the curve of her neck. His hands itched to reach out and test her skin. Was it as soft as he remembered? He breathed in her scent like a man who hadn't taken in fresh air for a decade. She smelled honey-sweet, warm and sultry. It was a nice, alluring contrast to the crisp mountain air outside.

"Now, that wasn't so bad, was it?" Sam whispered into her ear.

As if she'd been burned by a flame, she stepped away from him.

Earl's blue eyes twinkled with mischief. "Seein' you're going to the Cannadays' tree farm, might as well pick us up a fresh wreath for the front door. And maybe some mistletoe."

"Good idea," Sam said.

"We don't need mistletoe," Joy argued, the edges of her face reddening. "But I'll pick us up a wreath if that's what you want."

Joy took Lacey by the hand and led her to the door and out onto the snow-crusted sidewalk. Sam followed, but before he could shut the door, he heard the old gentleman say, "And mistletoe!"

Definitely not a bad idea, Sam thought, with his eye on Joy and his thoughts on how to make her his wife.

IT WAS A PICTURE-PERFECT scene right out of a Currier and Ives photograph. Spiky green evergreens dotted the smooth, rolling, snow-covered slopes. Tree boughs hung heavy with what looked like globs of thick white icing. Nestled deep in this valley at the Cannadays' tree farm, the mountains shielded shoppers from the bitter-cold winds. There was a joyous camaraderie among the townsfolk searching for the perfect Christmas tree. But the tranquil setting had the opposite effect on Joy.

Fastening the top button on her coat, she buried her nose in the wool scarf wrapped around her neck. Her insides crackled like ice splintering beneath warm water. What was wrong with her? Usually she enjoyed seeing her neighbors and friends out with their families and bundled up to their ears as they argued about whether a trunk was too crooked and sang carols slightly off-key.

The Jansens sped past on their snowmobile. The couple carried their two-year-old nestled between them. Joy's eyes filled with sudden unshed tears. She'd never been jealous of her friends' happiness before. And she wasn't now.

She touched a tender spot along her left side where the baby had jabbed her with its elbow. She was going to have a baby and she couldn't be more delighted. So why the tears? Why the bah-humbug mood smothering her spirits like a wet blanket?

Maybe Sam had been right. Maybe she was simply hormonal these days.

Determined to finish helping Sam and Lacey find their tree, then get back to the store to help Pop, she turned and caught sight of Lacey throwing a snowball at her daddy. The fluffy snow grazed his jeans-clad thigh. Lacey squealed and took off running.

Laughing, he crouched low and scooped up a handful of snow. His Stetson shaded his eyes, but his smile outshone the sun slanting on the powdery snow. For the first time since he'd arrived in Jingle and shaken her world to the core, she noticed his smile, its intensity, its power. How could she have forgotten its impact? After all, it had captivated her once. Without it even directed at her now, she felt a tightness seize her stomach. What was wrong with her?

More hormones, she decided. She didn't want Sam. She'd decided the night after they made love that he wasn't the man for her. And she rarely, if ever, changed her mind about something. But she had to admit he had a powerful effect on her. One she had to shake like a common cold.

Sam caught up to his daughter, hooking an arm around the little girl's waist and rubbing the disintegrating snowball against the front of her ski jacket. Lacey's giggles echoed through the valley, stirring something new and unique inside Joy.

Then Sam caught her watching them, studying them as if she were a distant outsider. He whispered something into Lacey's ear and the little girl started laughing. Together, they balled up more snow and started toward her.

"Oh, no you don't." Joy took a hesitant step backward, then bent low and made her own weapon, cupping the snow between her gloved hands.

Running and laughing at the same time, Lacey threw a snowball but it broke apart midair. Little bits of snow fell far short of Joy. "Get her, Daddy! Don't let her get away."

Don't let her get away. The words slammed into Joy. If only Sam hadn't let her get away that morning so long ago. If only he'd come after her, found her.

Then her life would be so different today. She'd still be pregnant, but she wouldn't be going through it alone. She would have had the love and support of Sam to comfort her in the dark, questioning hours of night.

But he hadn't cared enough. And she'd do well to remember that.

Sam didn't run toward her. He walked slowly, like a hunter gauging, assessing, stalking. His dark, hooded gaze held her spellbound. As he moved closer, he tossed the snowball in the air, catching it in the palm of his hand, re-forming it, then tossing it again and again as if he was toying with her.

"You wouldn't dare," Joy warned, wishing she'd run for the truck instead of standing her ground.

"Why not? Snow won't hurt you." He grinned, and a dimple creased one rugged cheek. "Or the baby."

"Sam, I'm warning you…"

He shook his head. "Get ready, darlin'. This cowboy may not know much, but I do know how to throw a snowball and hit my mark."

He knew a lot more than he gave himself credit for, she thought, like how to melt her insides with one look, or one simple kiss. But there was nothing simple or uncomplicated about kissing Sam. She didn't need a repeat performance to prove that to her!

She held out a hand to ward him off, all the while behind her back she held her own defensive weapon. "Sam, I mean it. Don't—"

"Don't what?"

Don't do this to me. Don't make me wish for things that can't be. We can't be a family. We can't.
"Don't throw that at me."

"I wouldn't think of it." He gave her a lazy, mischievous smile that tugged the corner of his mouth enticingly to the side.

Then he lunged for her. Before she could move out of the way, he grabbed her around the middle, firmly but gently, with one arm. In his other hand, he held the snowball, poised and ready to push it into her face.

They stood but a breath apart. His gaze locked with hers. Her heart pounded. Her breath caught. The heat simmering between them should have caused a flood as it melted the snow beneath them. He started to lean forward, to press the snowball closer, when his gaze dropped to her mouth.

He was going to kiss her.

And, heaven help her, she was going to let him.

Chapter Six

It was a mistake of gigantic proportions. Joy couldn't surrender to the insatiable desire. But she couldn't resist, either. She needed Sam's kiss, needed it like the mountains she loved, the comfort of her hometown that made her feel safe, the very air she breathed.

She would kiss him. This once.

Then she heard a dull splat. Sam inhaled sharply and hunched his shoulders forward. His features contorted. Ice crystals spattered the collar of his shirt. He clenched his teeth, and a shiver rocked through him. A well-aimed snowball had landed at the back of his head. Lacey's giggling laughter rang like tiny tinkling Christmas bells. Joy didn't know whether to be relieved or irritated. It would be a snowball's chance in you-know-where before she caved in again.

Taking advantage of Sam's shock, Joy snatched her opportunity and stepped out of his embrace.

He lifted one shoulder in an attempt to dislodge the icy ball, then cursed beneath his breath as more snow slid down the inside of his shirt along his spine. "Don't laugh."

Rolling her lips inward, Joy shook her head. When she'd gained a little control, she managed to say, "I wouldn't think of it."

"Don't forget I still have this." He held up a still-intact snowball.

"And I have this." She pulled an equal-size one from behind her back.

"Touché."

"I got you, Daddy! I got you." Lacey raced up to them, but kept a safe distance from her father. Unable to hide her ear-to-ear grin, she circled them, like a choo-choo train going around its track.

"You sure did, you little monkey." He brushed the rest of the snow off his neck.

Again, he shivered and yanked his shirt out from his jeans. Joy caught a glimpse of corded muscles along his stomach, and her skin tightened with unmistakable desire. When would she get him out of her mind?

When he left her life, she told herself. But how would she accomplish that?

"Ah, damn," Sam said, turning and brushing his hand along his back.

She started to reach out and brush away the remaining icy particles along his bronzed skin, but already the snowy bits were melting, making tiny rivulets along the smooth plane of his back. Instinctively...no, actually from experience...she knew one touch would avalanche her with too many emotions, too many untamed needs for her to control.

"I got you good," Lacey said, covering her mouth and another giggle with her mittened hands.

Grinning good-naturedly, Sam swooped down and scooped his daughter up in his arms. "You sure did, darlin'." He swung her around, turned her upside down, then settled her across his broad shoulder. Lacey's feet and arms dangled toward the ground. "Come on, let's go find that tree. It's waiting to get decorated."

Laughing and smiling, they trooped off toward a bank of evergreens to find their own tree. Sam placed his daughter on her feet, and the little girl grabbed her father's and Joy's hands. She skipped between them, singing "Jingle Bells" in the rhythm of her swaying arms.

The carefree energy bounding between them made Joy feel lighthearted, buoyant. Until she reminded herself that they were not a family. Not even a make-believe one. This wouldn't be *their* tree. It would be Sam's and Lacey's. Not hers. Not her baby's, either. The cold reality pinched her heart.

It took more than an hour for Lacey to find the perfect tree. Sam seemed to have the patience of a saint…St. Nicholas, that is. Of course, the only Santa Joy knew was her father. She'd always been impressed with Pop's ability to endure all the eager boys' and girls' questions, poking and prodding. He'd never seemed to tire of their chattering or of her badgering. She'd always wanted her child to have that same unconditional love.

Could Sam give that to their child? He obviously adored Lacey, doted on her, encouraged and loved her. Watching him with his daughter made Joy's chest tighten with longing.

But was that enough for a marriage to work?

No. Marriage required more. Much more. And she wouldn't settle for less. For her or her daughter.

Lacey circled dozens of potential trees before she settled on one. It had large, swooping branches and stood taller than Sam. With sure, powerful strokes, he began chopping the base. Joy settled herself on a tree stump and watched. Or tried not to watch.

His face was a mask of concentration, his jaw firm and solid, the muscles taut. The solid cracks of the ax biting into wood echoed through the valley and stirred old memories in her mind.

She remembered coming to this same tree farm as a little girl with her mother and father. It had always been a festive occasion with singing and frolicking. But the year after her mother died, Pop had quit bringing her here. He'd taken her to buy a pre-chopped tree from then on. Neither had wanted to face those painful memories. It had never been the same.

"Do you like it?" Lacey leaned against Joy.

She nodded. "It's beautiful."

"Are you gonna help us decorate it?"

Joy's breath caught. The sad fact was she'd been hoping to do just that. It was not a smart decision. She should be keeping far away from Sam. But she felt drawn to him and his daughter. It didn't make sense. In fact, it scared the starch right out of her spine. She felt him staring at her, the ax poised on his shoulder, as he waited for her response.

"Well, I don't know," she hedged, unsure of her

own emotions, uneasy with the chance she might be taking. Every moment she spent with Sam and his daughter, she began wavering on her decision not to marry him.

She reminded herself that parental love wasn't the glue needed for a strong, binding marriage. She needed and wanted more. Not just for herself, but for her child, who would benefit from a sound marriage as well.

"What if it don't look as pretty as your tree?" Lacey asked.

"It will." She looped her arm behind the little girl's waist. "Because you'll be decorating it. That will make it special and unique."

"But we only got lights. We don't have no ornaments."

"Any ornaments," Sam corrected her as he paused to catch his breath. Sweat beaded his brow. Swinging the ax to his shoulder, he readjusted his grip and began chopping again.

"How about if we make some?" Joy asked.

"Really?" The little girl's face brightened.

Was that a smile she saw curving Sam's mouth? Somehow that brought satisfaction. And pure pleasure. She nodded.

"Will you help?" Lacey lowered her voice and whispered, "I don't think Daddy knows how to do stuff like that."

"I'd be glad to."

At that moment, the base of the trunk cracked in two and the tree toppled over. The snow bank cushioned the fall. Hooking a rope through the bottom branches, he dragged the tree a few feet.

"Should work to get us back to the truck," he said over his shoulder. "Are you two ready to head back? How about a cup of hot chocolate?"

"Sounds good." Joy felt the cold numb her cheeks and hands.

Lacey rubbed her red nose with her mittened hand. "Don't forget we gotta get missy toe."

"Mistletoe." Sam's unnerving and unwavering gaze settled on Joy.

"What is it?" Lacey cocked her head toward her father for an explanation.

Sam scratched his jaw where a five o'clock shadow had begun to shade the hard, squared edge. "Well, it's a plant."

"A parasite actually," she corrected him.

He arched one eyebrow then narrowed his gaze on his daughter. "It's green with little white berries. Which you can't eat."

"People decorate at Christmastime with mistletoe," Joy explained. "Like they do with trees, holly and wreaths."

"Oh." Lacey's brow wrinkled as if she was mulling over these new facts.

"Folks hang the mistletoe above their front doors." His gaze slid toward Joy. "When someone stands under the mistletoe, someone else is supposed to kiss them."

Heat shimmied down Joy's spine, and she busied herself refastening one of the buttons on her coat.

"Why?" Lacey persisted.

"Tradition," Sam answered, his gaze darkening, making Joy's heartbeat quicken. "And we can't buck tradition, can we?"

"Nope." Lacey skipped ahead of them.

He waited for Joy to follow his daughter and fell into step with her, dragging the tree behind him. "I'm determined to make this a traditional Christmas for my daughter."

And family, she thought, unsure if he meant his statement as a threat or a promise.

"LET'S LEAVE THE TREE under the porch, until the snow melts off its branches." Sam set the cumbersome tree against the railing that encompassed his new ranch house.

It wasn't as fancy a house or as highly decorated as the one he'd shared with his ex-wife. Or should he say the one he'd paid for but rarely saw. But this ranch house, with its wraparound porch, had become home, even with its peeling paint that he intended to fix next spring and the sparse furnishings. His home. He'd never before felt as if he'd had a place of his own. But he was realizing it meant nothing without someone to share it with…like Lacey and his unborn child. A family…a real family…made it home.

"But Daddy—" Lacey started to whine.

"It won't take long to dry," Joy explained, stamping her feet on the welcome mat.

He'd been surprised when Joy hadn't put up an argument about coming here first. Well, surprised, relieved and anxious. If she accepted his marriage offer, then this would be her home, too. He hoped she liked it as much as he did. He hoped she saw its potential, rather than taking it at face value.

"By tomorrow," Joy continued, "you should be able to put your new tree up."

Lacey fought the frown turning the corners of her mouth downward.

"Then we can begin decorating." Sam cupped his daughter's chin affectionately.

Doubtful, Lacey looked to Joy, the expert.

She nodded in answer to the silent question. "Definitely."

"Then can we put up the missy toe now?"

"Uh, what about warming up with some hot chocolate?" Joy's cheeks looked suddenly pinker than before.

Sam gave a sly grin. He couldn't think of a better way to warm up than to kiss Joy. For some crazy reason that's all he'd been able to think about all afternoon. Maybe one kiss would get her out of his mind. But he doubted it. Taking her to his bed hadn't accomplished that, either. It had only made him want her more.

"Whatever you want, darlin'." He opened the front door and ushered his daughter inside.

Joy trailed slowly behind, edging around him so they wouldn't touch, and avoided his gaze. "This is nice. Large and roomy."

"For a big family," he said, noting the way her shoulders went stiff. *Back off. Don't push her too far or you might push her right out the door.*

After he'd helped Lacey hang her coat in the hall closet, he took Joy's, placing it alongside his own. For some strange reason, her gray wool coat looked as if it belonged there. The absurdity of that thought made him shake his head.

Taking a tack out of a desk drawer, Sam reached up to the door frame and hung the mistletoe they'd bought at the Cannadays' tree farm. Mrs. Cannaday had tied a pretty red ribbon around the stem. He had to admit it looked festive.

Turning back to his daughter and Joy, he said, "Now, who's gonna kiss me?"

"Me!" Lacey raced forward, hugged him around his legs and lifted her sweet face toward him. He kissed her gently. It never ceased to amaze him that he'd been given this precious gift. He never wanted to miss out on sharing things with his daughter. That's why he never wanted to fall in love again. He never wanted to be distracted from his purpose.

And Joy was definitely distracting.

But he could keep himself in check. He could shelter his heart, protect himself and Lacey. At the same time he was determined to convince Joy to marry him, so that his family could be complete.

"Now it's your turn," Lacey said, stepping away from him.

Joy's cheeks flamed as red as the ribbon on the mistletoe.

He smiled. Maybe a few kisses would help convince her marriage between them could work. Even if it wasn't the love-ever-after kind. "You're not going to buck tradition," he challenged, "are you?"

TRADITION. IT HAD ALWAYS meant so much to her family. Her parents had started many traditions when she was a small child, and her father had continued most after Joy's mother had died. She doubted Sam knew the true meaning of tradition.

But his challenge struck a chord in her. Or maybe it pulled her toward him. She edged forward, hesitant, wary. Not of Sam but of her own tempestuous feelings. Obviously the night they'd shared together hadn't meant anything but a physical release for Sam. And neither would this kiss. Well, two could play this game. She'd prove to herself and Sam that he meant nothing to her, either.

Fortifying herself against feeling anything but cool detachment, she boldly closed the gap between them. She'd make this kiss quick and easy. Maybe then she could move on with her life.

Just get it over with, Joy.

Then he touched her waist. A fluttering vibration started in the pit of her stomach. Through her thick sweater, she could feel his heat caressing her, making her resolve melt like sugar crystals in the rain. It made no sense. She was getting to be as big as a barn. She was pregnant, for God's sake! She wasn't supposed to feel aroused. She wasn't supposed to want to press her well-rounded body against Sam.

Sam! She certainly wasn't supposed to desire him!

He studied her mouth, as if trying to decide what kind of a kiss to give her. Long and slow? Cool and quick? A peck on the cheek? A chaste one on the mouth? Or a red-hot fiery one to remind them both of the night they'd shared? She was already warming up to the idea! Maybe she should back away. *Quick, before it's too late!*

Her heart skipped a beat with indecision. Her lips suddenly felt dry. She started to lick them, then stopped herself. He gave a tiny tug, pulling her closer, until her belly bumped against him and their breaths merged as one. She couldn't drag her gaze away from his. Something softened in his eyes, turning them gray and warm like a flannel blanket. *Don't look at him, Joy. Don't fall for a wink and kiss again. There's no promise in his eyes, no love.*

But she couldn't help herself. His gaze magnetized her. She couldn't have run if she'd wanted to.

As if in slow, erotic motion, he tilted his head, angling his mouth over hers. Her breath caught in her throat. She felt herself inching toward him, opening to him, willing him to kiss her fully and completely. *Oh, God, she'd lost her mind, her will-power, her heart!*

The phone rang, shattering the silence that had bound them. Jarred out of her trance, she blinked and started to step away, but Sam held her against him. The second ring jangled her nerves. The third made her want to scream.

"Lacey," he said, his voice husky, "could you get the phone?" He never took his eyes off Joy.

This time she couldn't keep from moistening her lips with the tip of her tongue.

"Sure, Daddy!" The little girl skipped toward the kitchen.

"Now," he said, "where were we?"

"You don't have to pretend with Lacey out of the room," she managed to say, despite her parched throat.

"I'm not pretending. I want to kiss you, Joy. Don't you remember what it was like?"

She remembered too well.

"Let me remind you."

Hold on for dear life. Here we go!

She struggled to maintain her aloofness as he pressed his mouth to hers, slanting his lips across hers. The instant his flesh touched hers a single spark flared into an explosion. The repercussions ricocheted through her body, firing her insides, sending shock waves down her spine, making her skin tingle. *What had she done?*

Why had she expected Sam to feel cold? He was warm and vibrant. His strong arms encompassed her in a titillating heat. Why had she expected him to be as tense and uncertain as she was? His touch was bold, confident, arousing. Of course, he didn't have a big pregnant belly. He didn't seem to have the same regrets she did. He seemed to take their new circumstances all in stride. How many women had he been with since her?

That thought struck her like a snowball smack in the face. She pushed away from him, her face burning, her body shaking.

"I don't need to remember anything about you…about that night. What's important is that it's over. This won't happen again." She swiveled on her heel and grabbed the door handle for support.

"Don't you want to stay for hot chocolate?" he asked, his voice vibrating inside her.

She yanked open the door and a cold blast of reality hit her as she picked her way across his porch, avoiding the patches of ice and snow. "Goodbye, Sam."

A deep chuckle brought her to a halt.

"What's so funny?" she demanded, glaring at him.

He dipped his head and rubbed his jaw. "Seems you forgot something."

No, she hadn't. She'd remembered his kiss all too well. It had been imprinted on her brain. And this reminder would haunt her as the others had already. It wouldn't matter if she was awake or asleep, she'd never be able to forget the feel of him, his gentle but daring touch.

"Your coat."

"Oh." Damn. Now she'd have to go back inside his house, feel the warmth, resist the attraction to Sam that she couldn't seem to put aside.

"And you don't have a car."

She blinked. "What?"

"It's a long way back to town." He called over his shoulder, "Come on, Lacey, we're going to drive Joy home." When he faced her again, his gaze was smoldering with invitation.

How did he make her—a mama-in-waiting—feel sexy and desirable? She reminded herself that he didn't want her. He wanted her baby. And he'd do anything to make her say yes.

Knowing she had no choice but to accept his ride back to town, she crossed her arms over her chest.

"Unless you've changed your mind about that hot chocolate?"

"No," she said, her lips pursed primly, "thank you."

SAM HID HIS STORMY emotions behind a carefree, nonchalant mask. He took pride in the fact that obviously their kiss had disconcerted Joy. Teasing her seemed appropriate and infinitely easier than admitting—even to himself—the way their kiss had shaken him to the core.

He wouldn't let a woman control him again. He wouldn't give into desire or insatiable needs that might distract him from his goal of being the best father to Lacey and this new baby.

It was the hope of sharing the birth and raising of this new baby that kept him from dropping Joy at her home, which was situated above the Christmas shop, and forgetting her completely. How could he forget the mother of his child? How could he walk away unscathed?

His determination to form a family forced him to remind her of her promise. He parked along Main Street, then alighted from his truck, skirting the front and opening the passenger door for Joy. "I'll pick you up tomorrow evening around six."

Her startled gaze lifted. "What?"

"Aren't you coming to help us decorate our tree?" Lacey asked. She'd been the buffer between them on the silent drive into town.

Hesitant, Joy glanced from his daughter to Sam.

"You promised," he whispered.

"So I did." She maneuvered herself out of the truck without taking his offered hand for help. "I'll drive myself."

He knew her reasons, understood and respected them. She was a self-assured woman. One, he reminded himself, who could break his heart.

LACEY GAVE A JAW-POPPING yawn but bravely dribbled more glue over the dough ornament.

"What color glitter do you want for that bell?"

Sam asked, giving a surreptitious glance at the clock above the pantry door. It was way past his daughter's bedtime. They'd eaten a hasty dinner of chili and corn bread that he'd spent all afternoon fixing, then they'd made several batches of dough ornaments.

This time, Lacey stifled another yawn but shrugged her indifference. She'd already made a gold, silver and blue bell. Her enthusiasm for the project had waned with each long hour.

"How about red?" Joy asked, trying to entice the little girl by adding an extra dose of perkiness to her voice. Obviously, she wasn't eager to be alone with Sam, either.

"How much more?" Lacey asked, her eyes starting to droop.

Guilt twisted inside Sam, but he hesitated to send her to bed. After all, if he did, then he'd be left alone with Joy to face the way she made him feel. How could a pregnant woman make him all jittery inside, like a schoolboy about to go on his first date?

Sitting together as a family seemed the right course of action. It provided a safe environment and maybe, just maybe, it would help convince Joy this was something their baby deserved.

"Just a few more ornaments," Joy said, reaching for a Santa-shaped one. "We'll be finished in a little while. Then tomorrow you and your daddy can decorate the tree."

"You're not going to help?" Lacey whined.

"Well..."

He'd have to change Joy's mind. Sam shoved

back the kitchen chair and stood. "I'll get the last tray of ornaments."

"You'll just have to slip a ribbon through the top of each ornament tomorrow after they've had a chance to dry," Joy said, her hands decorating as fast as she was speaking. "Then they'll hang on the tree perfectly."

Sam turned back to the table with the last cookie tray of ornaments. The sight of his daughter resting her head on the table pinched his heart. Her eyes were closed, her lashes shadowed her cheeks, her breathing slowed to a rhythmic pace. So much for well-laid plans. He slid the last batch of ornaments onto the table and said, "It's too late."

"What?" Joy looked up from her task.

"Lacey. She's bushed. I better put her in bed."

"Ah, poor thing. We worked her awfully hard."

Sam gave a grim nod. Carefully, he slid his arms around his daughter and scooped her into his arms. She weighed less than a sack of cattle feed.

"Do you need help?" Joy asked, pushing back from the table.

"You could open the door upstairs."

"Of course." She followed Sam up the stairwell. "You really do have a nice place here. It used to be the Martins'. They had to file for bankruptcy."

"I know, that's how I got such a good deal. It needs work."

"Just a little tender-loving care."

His gaze met hers and electricity sparked between them. He almost tripped on the top step.

Joy sidestepped around him. "Is her room down this way?"

"Third room on the right."

Neither turned on a light. They made their way down the darkened hallway. A night-light from the bathroom offered a haze of pale light. He carried his daughter to her pink canopied bed, and Joy folded back the ruffly covers. Gingerly, he laid her on the cotton sheets as Joy slipped off Lacy's tennis shoes. He had to admit they made a good team. He imagined what it would be like to put their baby to bed together in a few months. The image fueled his determination.

Tucking Lacey beneath the down comforter, he stood back and smiled down at his daughter. She didn't stir.

His daughter. It still gave him pause. Having a child still brought a lump to his throat. And soon he'd have another.

He looked at Joy. He had to convince her to join their family. There was no other acceptable option.

"I better be going," she whispered.

Touching her arm, he saw her eyes dilate. A sizzle of anticipation shimmied up his arm, jolting his heart. "Stay."

She took a step backward. "Sam, I can't. It's late. Pop will be worried."

"No, he won't. Stay and help me finish those ornaments."

"But…"

Lacey shifted beneath the covers, curling her body to the side. Sleepily, she sighed.

Sam tilted his head, indicating they should finish their discussion downstairs. When they reached the bottom landing of the staircase, he said, "I really appreciate all the help you've given us. I'm beginning to think I might just pull this Christmas off.''

"Of course you will. It's not as hard as you think.''

It was for a single father who'd never truly experienced Christmas, who didn't know the first thing about decorating a tree or house, who didn't know the right carols, who didn't feel comfortable in this family environment. "I couldn't have done it without you.''

Their eyes met, held. A warmth filled him from the inside out. A raw, aching need spread through his limbs, leaving him weak and awkward as a new foal. He knew there was more than one reason he didn't want Joy to leave. It unnerved him.

Joy glanced away first. She headed to the closet where he'd hung her coat. "I should be going.''

As she opened the closet door, he pushed it closed. She turned, and they stood but a breath apart. His heart bucked. Temptation pushed him, urging him to close that small gap between them and kiss her again. But it would be a mistake. Because he wasn't sure he could stop with one kiss. Anything more might frighten her away or make her angry. No, he had to play this very cautiously.

"Stay," he whispered, as if he might shatter the fragile truce between them. "I need your help.''

Almost a full minute went by before she answered, "Just until we finish the ornaments.''

Chapter Seven

The clock ticked loudly as the silence stretched between them. Joy ignored Sam's nearness—or tried to—and concentrated on decorating the dough-bread ornaments as quickly as possible. She wouldn't stay one minute longer than necessary.

"Would you like some coffee?" he asked, his husky voice intruding on her space, her peace of mind.

"I shouldn't. No caffeine during pregnancy." She placed a hand against her swollen abdomen to remind herself of the many reasons she shouldn't get involved with Sam. The baby gave a slight nudge with an elbow or foot and pushed her logical reasons out of the way. This baby was the best reason of all for Joy to establish a relationship with Sam. A lasting, intimate relationship, that is. But did Joy have to sacrifice everything—her hope for love, romance and a marriage like her parents had shared?

That night in Denver so long ago when she'd met Sam, she'd felt as if she'd known him forever. She'd seen the pain in his eyes from his divorce. But he hadn't been suffering a broken heart over the loss of his wife. No, he'd been in agony over the loss of his daughter. His raw emotions had struck a sympathetic chord. But now he seemed as remote and foreign to her as a Caribbean beach.

Sometimes she wondered how she'd been able to give herself totally to him. But when he looked at her with those overcast blue eyes, she knew. Because he still made her heart flutter, her stomach turn inside out and her skin burn for his—and only his— touch. No one else had ever made her yearn like Sam had...did.

"What else can't you have?" Sam asked, his deep, resonating voice startling her out of her wayward thoughts.

You. And no more kisses. Definitely no more intimate contact. She couldn't think straight with him near. He jumbled her thoughts and scattered her resolve. After the last kiss, as brief as it had been, she'd tossed and turned half the night trying to forget. Her body had almost glowed, teeming with a wild assortment of erotic feelings that couldn't be dimmed. They were more dangerous than intravenous caffeine injections. Maybe they were simply hormone-induced.

She shrugged, trying to keep the conversation light and casual, not delving into the real sacrifices she'd made or might have to make in the future for this baby. It didn't matter. "No artificial sweeteners, either."

"Hmm. Best to stick with good ol' Mother Nature, eh?"

That's exactly what had gotten her in this predicament!

Sam focused on her with what seemed like pin-point laser beams. Could he see through her facade? Could he sense the questions haunting her, confusing her? "You've had to give up a lot of your social life, too."

Her pulse skittered. What did he mean? Did he understand the real sacrifice it would take if she gave up her dream of a loving marriage for one of convenience? "Why do you say that?"

He gave a casual shrug, but there was anything but indifference in the straight line of his shoulders and the tension lining his mouth. "Charlie Foster."

His point-blank answer caused a bubble of laughter to rise in her throat, but his serious tone made her swallow it. Was he jealous? Or was he concerned she might give Charlie the honor of being her husband...and father to their baby? Sam wouldn't be concerned with anything but the latter. Irritation nettled her.

She gave a noncommital shrug. "Charlie's a wonderful man."

"Are you going to marry him?" His voice sounded strained.

She'd considered it during one panicky moment early on in her pregnancy. Charlie was a friend. He was solid, stable, a security blanket. But not the love of her life. So she'd gently turned him down even though he kept asking.

Why wouldn't she tell Sam outright that she wasn't going to marry Charlie or anyone else for the time being? Her spine stiffened. The answer was easy. It wasn't his concern.

Anger made her keep the words to herself.

Anger at Sam for not caring.

Anger at herself for caring too much.

"That's really none of your business," she snapped.

"Like hell." He shoved back his chair and glared at her. "The baby you're carrying is mine."

Her heart plummeted. She shouldn't have been surprised. But any secret fantasy she'd harbored that he might care whether she married someone else died a quick death. His concern was centered on the baby. *Her* baby. Not her. That realization sliced clean through her heart.

"What you do," he continued, "affects my baby."

"Our baby," she corrected him, meeting his heated gaze with one of her own. "So you want approval rights on who I spend the rest of my life with?"

"I offered to marry you."

She laughed then, a coarse sound. "Oh, yes! How could I forget? Such a gracious offer. One that I'm sure would make most rodeo groupies swoon with delight. But not me, buster. I'm not interested in the great sacrifice you're willing to make for our baby's sake."

He leaned back in his chair, crossing his arms over his chest. The plaid material pulled across his broad shoulders. "What are you so angry about?"

She shook her head with disbelief. "You're amazing, you know that? Would you like me to pick and choose who you get to marry?"

"I'm not the one carrying our baby."

"And just because I am you think that gives you

the right to run my life, to force me into a loveless marriage with you?''

His mouth thinned. A tick started in his temple. The veins along his neck swelled. ''When you put it that way, it sounds…well…you have to see where I'm coming from.''

''Oh, believe me, I do.''

''What's that supposed to mean?''

''Nothing.'' She stood and moved away from the table, needing a breath of fresh air.

But he grabbed her elbow and turned her back to face him. ''I'm sorry. I shouldn't have acted like a…a…''

''A Neanderthal?'' she offered.

The corner of his mouth twitched with half a smile. ''Well, I was thinking of something worse. But I'll settle for that. I deserve it.''

And more, she thought, her heart aching with the reality that he didn't want her. Not the way she'd wanted him. Past tense, she reminded herself. She didn't want him now.

''I could come up with a few other choice descriptions,'' she said, unable to suppress a wry smile of her own.

''It wouldn't be anything I haven't already said to myself.'' He stood too close, affecting her breathing, her heart from functioning properly. ''So what are we going to do?''

She gave a heavy sigh. ''We're going to go on living. Each day. Week. Month. We're going to have completely separate lives. You have your daughter. I have mine. Our paths will cross occa-

sionally. But they won't be parallel. Or inter-
twined.''

"I don't like that.''

"Well, I don't like giving up my coffee every
morning. But sometimes we have to do things we
don't like, Sam.'' God, she was starting to sound
like her father. "Get used to it.''

He flinched as if she'd struck him. His gray eyes
churned with a swirl of emotions she couldn't decipher. Slowly, he released her arm and stepped
away. "I know you think this should be easy for
me. I know you think I should just ride away and
forget...forget all we shared...forget that I helped
create that life inside you. But I can't.''

Her pulse pounded inside her ears. *Please, God,
don't let him propose again.*

His steady gaze held her captive, like iron chains
wrapped around her feet...and heart. "I respect you
for the decisions you've made, Joy. It can't be easy
facing the life of a single mother. It couldn't have
been easy admitting to your family and friends that
we made a mistake.''

Her heart stilled. Her spine snapped to attention.
"A mistake?'' She trembled with outrage. "Is that
what you consider this baby? A mistake?''

"Joy—'' He reached for her, but she batted away
his hand. "I didn't mean—''

"Well, I don't consider it a mistake. It's a bless-
ing. A rare and beautiful gift.'' She covered her
swollen belly with her hands. "This is a life...our
child...we're discussing, not the consequences to
some Truth or Dare game.''

He raised his hands in surrender. "Joy, I'm not

saying you should have done anything to correct the mis-mis…'' He shoved his fingers through his hair. ''Damn. I'm not doing a very good job of saying this.''

''No, you're not. I don't think I want to listen to any more. You're not the man I thought you were.''

He blew a frustrated breath between his parted lips. ''And you're not who I thought you were. Fact is, we didn't know each other well. I sure as hell didn't expect you to be the type to race out of my bed before the rooster crowed the next morning.''

The anger in his words whipped at her. She felt the burning truth. Things might have been different if she'd stayed. If she'd been patient. But she'd been frightened. Scared she'd made a mistake.

She held her arms across her stomach, pinching her elbows to suppress the trembling inside her. ''What are you trying to say, Sam?''

''That I think you're incredibly brave.''

His words stunned her, shook loose her bottled-up emotions. If only he knew what a coward she was. ''You're wrong.''

''I know a lot of women who would have taken the easy way out. And, well…thank you. Thank you for respecting the life we made together. Thank you for the sacrifices you've made…are making. Hell, I'm bungling this. I should just shut up. I guess I wanted to simply thank you.''

His words resonated with deep emotions and took her breath away. Honesty made his eyes shine like pure, liquid silver. Once again, a tingle of awareness rippled down her spine and weakened her knees, her resolve. This man continually surprised her. Why had she so devalued him? Why did she continue to do so?

"Must be strange having to accommodate your life for someone you haven't even met yet," he continued, tucking his fingertips inside the edge of his front jeans pockets and rolling back on his boot heels.

She knew he'd rearranged his life for his own daughter. Maybe if she'd given their relationship time, if she'd given him more than one night, then he might have done the same for her. But she'd never know that now. "We all make sacrifices one way or another. You certainly did with your daughter."

"I didn't do anything any other father wouldn't do."

"Sure you did. You quit the rodeo, your job, your life."

He ducked his head and studied the tips of his boots. "I would have quit a long time ago. If I'd had the chance. If I'd thought it would have saved my marriage."

"Didn't you love the rodeo?"

"It was the only family I'd ever known. But hell, it wasn't half as important to me as my daughter."

The force of his words tightened the strings of her heart.

"And I'm willing to make sacrifices again for this baby…our baby," he said.

Oh, no, we're not going there again. Feeling awkward with Sam's intense gaze focused on her and needing to change the topic quickly before he proposed again, before she capitulated, she turned and walked out of the kitchen and into the den. She stared at the plain green tree that Sam had erected in the corner. It tilted slightly to one side. It wasn't perfect, but then nothing in life was.

For many years she'd searched for the perfect tree each Christmas, checking the trunk, making sure each branch was full, each needle straight. She'd worked for days on decorating, stringing the lights carefully, placing each ornament on the right branch and spacing it far enough away from the others. She'd swagged gold tinsel along the branches and dangled silver icicles over the ends. The crowning touch had always been the shimmering angel at the top. Folks had always complimented her tree. But she'd seen the tiny flaws—gaps in the decorations, lights flickering too fast or too slow, even an awkward-shaped branch.

But looking at Sam's tree, knowing how long he'd worked to make it stand upright when all it had wanted to do was topple over, having seen the delight in Lacey's eyes, Joy knew this was the most beautiful tree. Not because of a spectacular array of ornaments. Not because of the latest chaser lights racing around the branches. Not because of the artistic design. But because it was surrounded by love. It made her think of home, of the trees her mother once decorated, of a time and place that she'd thought had vanished from her own reality.

"Looks a little precarious, don't you think?" Sam asked, his voice soft and low. He stood beside her, his arm almost brushing hers.

His nearness startled her. "I think it's beautiful."

"You're looking at it through Lacey's eyes."

No, she was seeing it through wisdom that came with pain and years of living. Like the trees of her Christmas pasts, she knew she'd judged Sam too harshly when she'd awakened by his side. She'd decided he wasn't the type of man she wanted, that he was a wanderer, a roamer. She'd wanted someone stable, someone who'd hang his hat beside her door each night. Someone like Charlie Foster?

No. She'd wanted someone like Sam. Someone who moved her. Someone who thrilled her. Someone whose touch made her wild with need. But she'd been too afraid to believe it was possible.

She looked at the tree in his living room through a veil of tears. "That's all that matters, isn't it?"

He nodded, then seemed to notice her emotional state. Turning to face her, he said, "Are you okay?"

She sniffed. "Hormones." Nodding toward the tree, she said, "It reminds me of the Christmases I had as a little girl."

"Must have been pretty spectacular."

"More homey, I'd say. But special nonetheless. There was always an abundance of love."

Sliding his gaze back toward the tree, he said, "I wanted it to be perfect. For Lacey. For our first real Christmas together. But I don't know the first thing about decorating a tree."

"It's not that difficult."

"Maybe for you. I don't even know what to put on first. The star at the top?"

Joy looked at him as if with a new set of eyes. Smiling, she said, "How do you get dressed?"

Humor turned his eyes a smoky blue. "Excuse me?"

"I m-mean," she stammered, feeling her face burn. "The star should go on last. Like your hat. Don't you put your Stetson on last when you're getting dressed?"

"Usually."

"Well—" she crossed her arms over the top of her rounded stomach, embarrassed by her slip of the tongue "—it's the same."

He turned his attention back to the tree, and she was able to draw a deeper breath. "So, if the star is symbolic for my hat, then what's my belt buckle?"

The heat from her face flared, flaming along her neck and chest. "The tinsel."

"Ah. And the lights?"

"Your...uh..." A flashing memory of Sam without his shirt—his bronzed muscles bare, his abdomen taut—sent an electric charge through her. Then she remembered what he looked like without his jeans, without his B.V.D.s. *Oh, heavens!* "Uh, the lights go on first."

"On the bare limbs?" He smiled, making the corner of his mouth dent his cheek.

"Yes." She kept her gaze averted, but she knew he was teasing her.

"The ornaments go on after that?"

"Uh-huh." She fluffed the end of a branch. "Nothing to it, really."

"I doubt that."

"It really doesn't matter what order you do it in," she said, pretending to study the tree from another angle.

"Wouldn't want to go out in public with my underwear showing. Would you?"

"No, but…whatever you do will be fine. As long as Lacey likes her tree."

Chuckling to himself, he said, "You're right."

"Haven't you ever decorated a tree before?" she asked, wishing she'd taken the lull in the conversation and said good-night instead of pursuing this. Hadn't she learned her lesson already? She should never have compared a Christmas tree to getting dressed. Where had that thought come from?

He shook his head. "Never dressed a tree. Never chopped one down till yesterday. Never made a bunch of ornaments or anything else festive, for that matter."

Her jaw dropped slightly but she recovered quickly. "How come?"

It was his turn to keep his gaze trained on the tree. When he spoke, his voice was low, introspective. "I only remember having one tree as a kid. A pathetic silver one. It sat in the corner of the den for six or seven months after my mother walked out on us. Finally, my dad tossed it out.

"Never had a tree at Christmas after that until I got married. Then I was always on the road at rodeos or wrangling cattle up until Christmas. The decorating was all done by the time I got home." He gave a hoarse huff. "Home. Strange word for some place that felt more alien than a part of me."

"Why was that?" she asked, intrigued by the wounds he'd suffered yet amazed by his gentleness. But she felt something more. She cared for this man, cared for him in a way that caused her to feel his pain.

His posture looked stiff, as if he were frozen in the grief he'd felt as a child. "It doesn't matter."

"It does to me." She wanted to soothe his brow, ease the strain from his face, the tension from his shoulders. But she didn't dare.

He shoved his hands into his back pockets. "It was probably my fault. I was gone all the time. I felt more at home on the road."

"You don't seem that way here."

He looked at her then. His eyes looked cloudy, then cleared like a summer day. "You're right. It's not much of a place. I have a lot to fix up. A lot I want to do. But this is home. I feel it in my bones. It's something I've never felt before."

He grew silent, contemplative. This strong man had a tender, emotional side. It was his vulnerability that made her behave recklessly, like a woman in love. It made her want to reach out to him now.

Restraining herself, using her logic rather than her emotions, she kept her hands to herself. The silence made her aware of the ticking of the clock on the mantel. Finally, she probed further. "What was your home like growing up?"

He looked up at the wooden planks along the ceiling. "As different from Jingle as heads and tails on a penny."

"How so?"

"Jingle's a family-oriented town. Family means something here. Traditions belong here."

She cocked her head to the side. "Your family didn't have traditions? No regular holidays they celebrated. No—"

"I didn't have a family. After my mother walked out, my father left every chance he could."

Her heart contracted as she imagined a scared, lonely little boy searching for a family. No wonder he was determined to make Lacey's Christmas the best ever. He needed it for himself, to fill an empty space in his own life. "Who raised you then?"

"I did."

"But..." She shook her head, not understanding how a parent could go off and leave his child. "So you and your father didn't celebrate Christmas together?"

"Not the way you do. Let's just say, he celebrated. Every Friday, Saturday...most nights of the week. And Christmas was no exception."

She studied Sam's profile, the stern outline of his proud forehead, his jutting, determined jaw. "Without you?"

"I had chores to do on the little place we called a ranch. It wasn't but a few acres. But it was all we had. Our house was about the size of a henhouse. On most nights, especially holidays, my father went to the local tavern and kicked up his heels, drank himself into a stupor. I'd get a call sometime past midnight to come pick him up and carry him home. That was our big Christmas celebration."

"Oh, Sam..." Her throat clogged with emotions. Her eyes filled with tears.

"Don't feel sorry for me. Not everyone has what you grew up with. It's okay. I'm over it."

But was he? She knew then he needed the Christmas as much as his daughter. And she was going to see that he got it. "I'll help you make this Christmas what you want it to be."

His look told her more than words could communicate. It made her feel buoyant, light, knowing that she was going to help him. Not just Lacey, but Sam.

Then she'd have to step away and let them live their lives. As she went on with her own.

She glanced at the clock. "I should be going. It's getting late."

He nodded. "You need your rest. Will you be okay driving back by yourself?"

"Of course."

"Will you call me when you get home? Just so I know you're okay."

Her heart snagged on hope. Was he concerned about her welfare…or their baby's? If only… No. She wouldn't let herself think that. She knew that Sam would never give his heart away. It had been shattered long ago. "I'll get my coat."

"Joy?" The plea in his voice stopped her, made her turn back toward him, anticipation welling inside her.

"Yes?" What if he asked to kiss her? What if she couldn't say no?

"Could I…would you mind if…" He cursed beneath his breath. "Can I touch the baby…our baby again?"

Her heart sagged with the weight of reality. When would she learn? When would she resist the temptation to hope that there could be something more than this baby between them? She couldn't disregard his question, nor could she tell him no. At least he cared about their baby. At least she had that much to hold on to. It was better than if he'd abandoned her, taken her rejection and run. Wasn't it? Sometimes she wasn't so sure which was more painful to endure.

"It's okay."

He took a hesitant step forward. "Where do I..."

"Give me your hand," she said. When their fingers touched, she tried to ignore the quiver in her belly. Slowly, she placed his hand against her abdomen. His touch was gentle but firm. He shouldn't make her feel this way, shouldn't make her feel tingly and aroused. But he did.

Trying to keep her mind off his nearness, off his broad shoulders and strong hand, she said, "You can talk to the baby. If you want."

"Talk to it?" His brow furrowed. "You mean, she can hear me?"

"Sure."

He leaned down until his face was inches from her belly. The lights overhead picked up a hint of brown in his wavy hair. She could have run her fingers through its thickness, but once again she resisted, curling her fingers into her palm and holding tight.

Clearing his throat, he said, "Uh, hello there...baby." He glanced up at Joy. "Have you named her yet?"

The sparkle in his eyes made her throat close. She shook her head.

He smoothed his hand along her stomach, which made even her toes tingle. "This is your daddy."

He straightened, his ears turning red at the tips. "I feel silly."

"It's okay." She covered his hand splayed across her belly. "I understand."

He cupped her face and drew a path along her jaw with his thumb. "Thank you."

"For what?"

"For sharing this with me. For having my baby." Then he kissed her.

It was a light, fluttery kiss, but its impact was powerful and earth-shattering. As quickly as his lips touched hers, he moved away.

"I'll get your coat."

She nodded, unable to speak, unable to move. *Don't do it, Joy. Don't fall for Sam again. It can't work. It can't be as magical as you want. Not when you'll never own his heart.*

Chapter Eight

A snowstorm blew through the following afternoon, making the roads impossible to travel. The schools closed for two days, and Sam struggled to entertain his active five-year-old daughter in between checking to make sure there was enough hay and water for the cattle.

The following Saturday when Joy knocked on their door, he'd never been so relieved to see another adult in his life. Her cheeks were rosy from the bitter wind, her auburn hair tousled and her blue eyes vivid and shining.

"Come on in," he said, well aware of the mistletoe above his head. This time he refused to consider the possibility of a kiss. Joy's smile warmed him from the inside out, buffeting the Colorado chill, making him want to ignore the restrictions he'd placed on himself. "I wouldn't have minded picking you up."

"No sense you driving to town and then back." She shrugged out of her coat, and his gaze automatically sought her rounded stomach, which protruded beneath her bulky sweater like a basketball.

Pride bounded inside him. "But I can't stay long, so let's get busy. Where's Lacey?"

"Here I am!" His daughter bounded into the entryway.

That morning, she'd asked him to put her hair in pigtails like Marcy Ann Baker's. He'd tried, but frankly she looked lopsided. A mama cow could have done a better job. His fingers still ached from those coated rubber bands he'd twisted around clumps of her hair. But at least she was well coordinated, wearing a matching red shirt, blue corduroy jumper and navy shoes. He'd been told by his ex-wife that matching outfits were important to little girls.

"We already put the lights on." Lacey bounced from foot to foot.

"Yep," Sam said, with a knowing look in Joy's direction, "we put the tree's underwear on."

A tinge of red brightened her temples, and she averted her gaze.

Giggling, Lacey grabbed Joy's hand and pulled her into the den. "Come look."

"Oh, how wonderful!" Joy exclaimed, looking more at his daughter than the wobbly green tree with lights that seemed to chase one another around each limb at breakneck speed. "So beautiful."

"Think so?" Lacey asked.

"I know so." She knelt beside his daughter and placed an arm around Lacey's waist. "Now we need to add the tinsel and ornaments. But remember, we have to be careful. We don't want to break any. They're fragile."

"I'll be careful."

Sam gave an inward self-affirming nod. He'd be careful, too. With his heart.

Two hours later, the tree's branches bowed beneath the ornaments, lights, tinsel and icicles. Sam reached the top and placed the star at the apex. His heart quickened at the joy on his daughter's face, and he mouthed a heartfelt "thank you" to the woman who'd made it all possible.

Blinking, Joy gave a quick nod of understanding and turned away. She stretched, arching her lower back, and glanced at her wristwatch. "I better get going."

"Do you need to get back to the store?" Sam asked. "Things are probably picking up with Christmas just around the corner."

"Pop's cold is better," she said, "but things are hectic."

"Do ya gotta help Santa get ready for Christmas?" Lacey asked. She held up a piece of construction paper that had a green-and-red chain attached. "Only twenty-one more days. I bet he's got lots to do."

"Yes, he does." Joy gave a soft maternal smile that had Sam's heart contracting. She'd make a good mother to their child. But also to Lacey. Now, if he could just get her to say "I do."

"And we have lots to do ourselves." He ruffled his daughter's hair. "Like buy presents and—"

"Presents!" Lacey bounced in place. "Can we get Joy something, too, Daddy?"

"Sure we can—"

"That's not necessary."

Sam's gaze collided with hers. Was she always

going to be this difficult? But then he'd given her all she probably ever wanted from him...their baby.

At that moment, the doorbell rang.

"Who could that be?" Sam asked, tossing an empty box in the trash.

"Probably Charlie." Her answer stopped him cold.

"Charlie? That guy I met in your shop?"

"Yes. He brought me out here, and we'd prearranged for him to pick me up—" she shifted her gaze away from him, back to her watch "—about now." She gave him an awkward smile.

His insides twisted with a surreal emotion. Jealousy? Anger? Irritation? Well, of course, irritation. What if they hadn't finished by their "prearranged" time? *You can't take up all Joy's time, McCall.* Anger fit, too. After all, Charlie had made no secret of the fact that he was trying to marry Joy. That right belonged to Sam. Didn't it? After all, she was carrying *his* child, not Charlie's. Which led him to his final conclusion about the strange emotions pummeling his insides.

Jealousy! Joy shouldn't be hanging out, driving around with, or seeing another man. Not when Sam, the father of her baby, was around and more than willing to save her reputation. Not when he needed...wanted her to marry him!

"Joy—"

"Charlie's waiting." She grabbed her coat and shoved her arms into the sleeves before he could offer to help. "Bye, Lacey. Enjoy your tree."

"Bye," his daughter said, her lip protruding a smidgen.

"Bye, Sam," Joy said, reaching the door.

But it wasn't goodbye. Not by a long shot. It was just the beginning. Joy had better face that fact soon. Sam was determined. And getting in front of a determined cowboy was as dangerous as standing in the path of a rank, angry bull.

AFTER PACKING UP her customer's purchase, Joy gave a weary smile to her customer. "Thank you for stopping by, Mrs. Johns."

"Let me know when that singing wreath comes in. My Ed just rolls with laughter every time he sees one of those."

"Yes, ma'am. We should have those in any day." She tried to maintain her smile even though the silly decoration Sally Johns had ordered made her groan. She preferred less commercial decorations and homemade ones even more. Like the ones she had helped Sam and Lacey make.

Oh, no, Joy! Don't even go there. Quit thinking about him!

It was easier to think about her aches and pains at the moment. She sank onto the stool behind the front counter. Her feet were swollen, her back had a catch in it and the baby was using her stomach like a punching bag. It was only ten-thirty in the morning, but already this had been a record-breaking and back-breaking Monday morning.

"Bye-bye," Sally called over her shoulder.

"Have a merry Christmas."

Turning to brace her back against the cold wind, Sally waved and tucked another package under her arm. "You, too, my dear. Looks as if it's going to be a cold one this year. Keep that baby warm."

Actually the baby was keeping her toasty. Nodding her agreement, Joy was relieved that the freezing weather wasn't one of her complaints today. The cold and snow didn't seem to bother her at all this year. But something else did.

Closing the register drawer, she heard the jingle of the bell above the door as Mrs. Johns carried her bundles outside. A shadow crossed her face, and she looked up to greet another customer ready to check out.

"Will that be all?" she said automatically, but the last word stuck in her throat.

Sam. The something—or someone—who had been bothering her for the last couple of weeks had walked into her shop again. Couldn't he leave her alone? She'd hoped on Saturday when she'd left his ranch that she wouldn't see him for a while...if not longer. After all, she had helped him and Lacey with their tree. What more did he want?

Instinctively, she knew. Automatically, her hand touched her stomach. "Where's Lacey?"

"School."

"Oh." It made her nervous being in the same room—alone—with Sam. Well, okay, they weren't totally alone. There were a few customers milling around. Still, her pulse raced and her insides jumbled together in an odd mixture of dread and anticipation. "What can I do for you then? Need some outside lights to spruce up the ranch?"

"Not today."

Giant butterflies paraded through her stomach.

"Grady Department Store down the street is having a sale on dolls. Maybe Lacey would like one for her present this year."

"That's an idea. But I'm not out shopping right now."

"No?"

He shook his head and hers began pounding. "I didn't come for your help."

"You didn't?"

His eyes were the color of charcoal, dark and smoldering. "I came to help you."

"Me?" She almost strangled on a peculiar emotion wedging in her throat.

He came around the edge of the counter, crowding her, making the small space behind the register seem even tinier. "You shouldn't be working so hard. You need to rest, relax, take care of yourself and the baby."

She bristled and lifted her chin. "I am."

"Good." He gave her a disarming smile that took the starch right out of her, leaving her weak-kneed. "And I'm here to take care of you."

Her heart contracted. If only... No, she wouldn't fall for a line like that. She knew why he was here. "Sam, I don't need your help. I'm perfectly capable of taking care of myself and my...our baby."

"Then humor me." He touched the corner of her mouth. "And smile once in a while. It's Christmas. Besides, you look beautiful when you smile."

A frown pinched the space between her brows. What was he up to now?

Before she could ask him, a customer picked that

moment to approach the counter. "Could you tell me where the indoor lights are?"

"Sure." Joy stood. Her shoulder bumped Sam's arm. With him standing back here, there was barely enough room to maneuver. Standing so close to him made her pulse skitter and dance crazily. She tried to sidestep around him, but he clasped her shoulders.

His look was steady, sincere and brooked no argument. "You stay put. Take a load off." He doffed his Stetson and laid it on the counter beside the register. "I'll show the lady where the lights are."

Focusing his attention on the waiting customer, he said, "It's your lucky day, ma'am. I'm practically an expert in the lights department."

Joy lifted her hand to voice a protest, but the woman smiled coyly at Sam and followed after him like a puppy dog on a leash.

Leading the woman toward aisle number four, he said, "Now, were you looking for chaser lights, which happen to be my favorites? Or were you looking for some lights that play Christmas carols, too?"

With a sigh of resignation, Joy let her reservations take a back seat to the sudden desire to rest. She watched with amusement as Sam helped customer after customer, encouraging them to buy more items than they'd intended. Pleased, Joy rang up their purchases.

As the morning waned, so did her resistance to Sam's charm. She found herself smiling at the jokes he told her customers. She laughed at the way he placed a fake Santa beard over his face. She rolled her eyes with amusement when he put a twinkling star on the top of his head to show a customer how it would look on top of a Christmas tree. As her attraction escalated, her nerves frayed.

Finally, she decided she'd had enough. But with the store crowded as folks took their lunch breaks to browse through the shop, she couldn't fire Sam. Especially when she'd never hired him! The simple solution was to find something for him to do somewhere else, where she wouldn't have to listen to him enchant female customers with his down-home charm. She sent him to the back to unload some boxes from the delivery truck. At least it spared her and Pop from having to do the heavy labor themselves.

But even out of sight, he wasn't out of her mind…or heart.

Her emotions felt all scattered. Sam's consideration was sweet. Even if it was only for their baby. Not her.

Why did that thought continue to nettle her?

At lunch he weathered the cold and brought her back a turkey sandwich and coleslaw from the deli down the street. He set the table in the back and filled her glass with water. "Joy, you need to eat. I'll watch the front."

"But, Sam—"

He wouldn't listen to her arguments. "Gotta keep your strength up."

"But what about Lacey? Your ranch?"

"Lacey is going to a new friend's house after school. And I can take care of the ranch and help you, too. I'll do my chores, feed the cattle, check fences, early in the morning and late at night."

"But you don't know how to run the register."

"What's to know? It's not like it's high tech. And if I hit a snag, I'll call you. Now, eat. Customers are waiting."

She felt uncomfortable letting him take charge and order her around, much less ask him to do chores for her, but she couldn't deny that it felt awfully good to sit down for lunch. Just this once. After all, she couldn't let Sam come in here every day. He'd drive her crazy. And her hormones were already on a rampage.

Besides, her back was feeling better. Maybe she just needed a little rest today. She'd be fine tomorrow. Or maybe she'd let Sam help every now and then. What could it hurt? It wasn't as if she was going to marry him to show her appreciation.

After enjoying a few leisurely minutes eating her lunch without the constant barrage of customers' questions and demands, she ambled back to the front. Sam was helping Edna Warren out to her car with an artificial tree. She couldn't help noticing the bulge of his muscles straining the seams on his flannel shirt and his taut backside beneath those jeans. He wrestled the heavy box into the woman's trunk as if it were a squirming calf. His hands were sure and strong as he tied a rope to secure Edna's trunk from flying open. When he reentered the store, his face was chafed from the wind, his eyes light as the gray clouds overhead, his hair tousled and sexy. She had to quit thinking like that!

"Mrs. Warren bought an artificial tree?" she asked, trying to divert her attention away from Sam. "She's been eyeing one for years but never has purchased one."

"Guess I have a salesman's touch," he said with a wink and a smile.

"Well, I better order some more. If Edna bought one, then her bridge group will all be in next week wanting the same one."

Sam laughed. "Want me to catalog it for you?"

"Sure," she said. "The sheet is in the back office on a clipboard."

"I'll get it. Anything else you need?"

"Not right now. I'll keep an eye on the register."

Watching him walk back to her father's office, she felt a pinch in her chest. She remembered her mother and father working this way together. But between little discussions like she'd just had with Sam, her folks had shared kisses and hugs. It had been a friendly, loving atmosphere. It's what she'd always imagined one day for herself—a marriage to someone who was strong and sure enough to love unconditionally and brazenly.

That's not what Sam is offering, Joy. He only wants this baby. He doesn't want you. He won't give you his heart.

And she wouldn't marry him...or anyone else for that matter...without the necessary ingredient of love.

"I was thinking," Sam said, returning to the front a few minutes later.

Here we go, she thought, back to the marriage conversation.

"You could probably update your system," he said, "make it more efficient, less of a hassle."

Her spine stiffened. She realized it had been a while since he'd mentioned marriage. Why did that irritate her? Why should he continue to ask her when she'd said no loud and clear? And why did she want him to keep hassling her? It made no sense.

What made even less sense was for Sam to barge into her life and start telling her what to do—how to eat, when to rest, who to marry, or who not to, and now how to run her shop! "You don't know what you're talking about, Sam."

He gave a slight pause and rubbed his jaw. "I agree I'm more knowledgeable in cattle. I sure don't mean to pry. But I run a business, too. I've been thinking of updating, myself. This is the beginning of a new millennium. Whoever said an old cowboy couldn't learn a new trick?

"I've got a friend in Wyoming who just bought himself one of those new-fangled computers. He's logging in his cattle, keeping track of them that way, advertising his bulls on the Internet. I was thinking it might be a lot easier for you, what with the baby coming, to keep track of your stock if you were to do that."

She felt walls of resistance lift around her heart and mind. "Pop wouldn't agree."

"He might. He's progressive."

"He wouldn't."

Sam leaned against the counter. "The store will be yours someday. You could do it then."

"No." Tension tightened her jaw.

"You won't even think about it?"

Her face burned with a rush of inexplicable emotions. "No."

"But—"

"No, Sam. End of discussion." She swiveled off

the stool and stalked past him to the office. Her eyes stung with unshed tears. Her chest ached. She needed a minute alone to get her emotions under control. What was wrong with her?

First she was angry that Sam wasn't asking her to marry him. Which was ridiculous! Now she was bawling when he tried to make her job easier. It made no sense. But still she couldn't stem the flow of tears. Her shoulders shook. Her throat burned.

"What did I say that was so wrong?"

She swung around, shocked to find he'd followed her. "Forget it, Sam. Let it go." *Let me go.*

But she knew a part of her didn't want him to do that. Was she testing him? Trying to see what his limits were?

He touched her arm, his thumb caressing her skin, triggering electric sparks along her spine. "Whatever it was," he said, his voice deep and full, "I'm sorry."

She shrugged, trying to ease away from him, but at the same time wanting to lean into him. "It's no big deal."

"If I made you cry, then it is."

She sniffed and reached for a tissue on her father's desk. "I do this all the time."

"You do?"

Nodding, she said, "Hormones."

"Oh." He gave her a quizzical look. "Sure I didn't say something that prompted it?"

"Maybe. But it's no big deal."

He took her by the shoulders and turned her around to face him. His eyes were dark and stormy with raw emotions, reminding her of that first night she'd met him, the night she'd fallen in love with him. "Tell me."

She sighed. "Sam—"

"I didn't mean to hurt you, Joy. Tell me so I won't do it again."

"It's just that this is my mother's store. This is the way she set things up. This is the way we've always done it. And, and..." Tears filled her eyes.

He pulled her against him. "And I trod on sacred ground."

His strength and warmth soothed her frazzled nerves. She knew there was more to her tears than what she'd told him. There were her chaotic feelings for him that she'd battled all day with him near. But she wasn't about to confess them.

"I'm sorry, Joy. Can you forgive me?"

"You didn't know."

"I shouldn't have barged in and taken over."

A smile tugged at her lips. "You did sort of, didn't you?"

He nodded. "I'm sorry."

"I'm not."

He raised an eyebrow. "Really?"

"I was tired. And you really helped me today. Thanks."

"You're welcome. And I'm going to go right on helping."

Until you have our baby. She could almost hear his words. She flinched at his reasons. But she figured it could be worse. At least he cared about their baby. Even if he didn't care about her.

"Joy—" he cupped her chin, his metallic gaze magnetizing her "—I want you to marry me."

Why did the words sound hollow? She pulled away from him. "Sam, I told you no and I meant it."

"But—"

Maybe if he understood what she wanted, he'd run for the hills. Isn't that what she wanted? "Look, I grew up watching my parents love each other and run this store together as a team. They were perfect together, always helping, always glowing when the other was around. But then my mom died. And things changed. One thing that hasn't ever changed is this shop. It has kept her memory alive.

"And one of the things I remember and have always wanted is the kind of marriage my parents had." She placed a protective hand over her belly. "I won't give my baby anything less than what I had growing up—parents who adore each other. If that's not possible, then I'll go it alone."

"You know that's impossible, don't you?" he asked, his face dark with anger.

"I know it's impossible for you to love again. You've made that clear."

"So you're saying there's someone else? That Charlie?"

"I'm not saying anything." She crossed her arms over her chest.

"You and I are the baby's parents. That's why we should be married."

"No, Sam, it takes more than that. Much more. And I won't cheat myself or this baby. It's love or nothing."

Chapter Nine

The following day Sam parked his truck outside Joy's shop before she'd even switched the sign in the frost-covered window to read Open. He'd realized yesterday that she needed his help desperately. Hell, he wasn't a knight in shining armor, but he could ease her burdens. If she'd just let him!

No matter what she said, he was also determined to marry her. For their baby's sake. Too bad if Joy had some pipe dream stuck in her head. She'd have to get over it. And fast. They were running out of time. It wouldn't be long before their baby arrived.

She had to understand that their child deserved both a mother *and* a father. If that meant a secure but loveless marriage, then so be it. It was a helluva lot better than her plan!

Besides, he wasn't giving his heart to anyone. He'd tried that once and almost lost his daughter and heart in the bargain. Not again. Now he had his priorities straight. Romance wasn't at the top of his list. It wasn't even at rock bottom. Being the best father was number one. Lacey and the new baby would be his main focus.

With a determined stride, Sam pushed open the shop door and heard the now familiar jingle of bells above his head.

"Mornin'." Earl looked up from the register.

Sam gave a grim nod, his cheeks still cold from outside. "How are you feeling, sir?"

"Better every day I can get down here and putter around." He lifted a hefty mug of coffee and sipped the contents, grimacing as he swallowed. "If you're looking for Joy, she ain't here."

Perplexed, Sam shut the door behind him and moved toward the front counter. "Did she have a doctor's appointment?"

"Nope. She said she was feeling tired and wanted to sleep in. I thought it was a good idea, seein' she's been working so hard lately to carry the burden of the shop on both her shoulders."

Concern straightened his spine. He looked toward the stairs that led to the Chase's home upstairs. "Should I go check on her?"

"Ah, she's okay, son. Give her time."

Time! Time? No one seemed to notice how time was running out, as Joy's belly expanded and the delivery of their baby approached. Time was of the essence if they were to get this settled before then.

Sam jerked off his Stetson and slapped it against his thigh. "I don't have the time."

Earl frowned and set his mug on the counter. "We talkin' about two different things here?"

He gave a grim nod. "It's no secret that I'm trying to talk your daughter into marrying me."

"I know." Earl's bushy white eyebrows slanted

into a V, making him look more like Ebenezer Scrooge than Santa Claus.

"And?"

"It's her decision."

Sam shook his head. "She's bullheaded."

Earl laughed, transforming his face suddenly from discontentment to agreement. "That she is."

Leaning against the counter, Sam asked, "Why do you think she's so resistant?"

The older gentleman scratched his beard. "Well, what are you offering?"

"What do you mean? Marriage. Security. A name for her baby."

"She's got her own name. Nothing wrong with Chase. And she's got plenty of security in her own bank account and in the future of this shop. Looks to me, young fellow, that you've got to offer something more, something enticing."

"Like what?"

"Romance."

Sam curled his lip with disgust.

Earl raised his hand. "Now, listen. What woman wants to accept a marriage proposal that only promises security and a good name? Not one. At least not in this day and age. Heck, women have seen too many of those Hollywood movies."

"And read too many of those romance novels," Sam added with a scowl.

Nodding, Earl continued, "They want love. They want to hear wedding bells chiming in their ears, for their heart to palpitate, for some gorgeous hunk to want them above all others."

Sam stared down at the tips of his boots. What

the hell did he have to offer a woman like Joy? He was a man who lived a simple ranching life. A man who wore jeans and boots and preferred quiet evenings to rip-roaring paint-the-town-red nights. A man with a daughter and another on the way.

For God's sake, that should be enough! He was her baby's father.

"If you want to marry my daughter," Earl said in a conspiratorial tone, "then you're going to have to do a little old-fashioned courting."

"Courting?"

"Woo her."

"Woo?"

"Oh, brother. You need more help than I thought."

Courting? Wooing? He didn't have time for romance. He had a baby on the way. And what would romance get him, anyway? That gave him pause. It might just get him a wife…Joy. If it would, then he was just desperate enough to try it.

"I know what you mean."

"Good. I was beginning to wonder how you got my daughter in this predicament in the first place."

The tips of Sam's ears burned. He knew all about *that* kind of romance. This time, he'd keep his heart out of it and use his brain instead. Hadn't he read that was the most important lovemaking organ? Wouldn't hurt to give it a try. Better than involving his heart.

Resting his hands on the counter, Sam leaned toward Joy's father. "Would you be willing to help me out? It's for a good cause."

"How do you figure that?"

"I'm looking out for your daughter and grand-daughter." He let the impact of that wallop the older gentleman.

Earl met Sam's direct gaze, his blue eyes narrowed to slits. "You better treat her right. Both of 'em. Understand?"

"Yes, sir."

"And iffen you don't, then you've got me to answer to." He patted his belly. "Don't let this fool you. I can be hard and mean when I have to. I don't want you trifling with my daughter's heart. She's already been through enough. So what will it be?"

Sam stuck out his hand. "You don't have anything to worry about, sir."

Shaking on their agreement, Earl said, "Good. What can I do?"

WELL PAST NOON, Joy decided the coast was clear and made her way down to the shop. She'd seen Sam arrive early that morning and not much later he'd returned to his truck and driven away. She hadn't seen hide nor hair of him since. And she didn't plan to. Now it was time for her to relieve her father.

"How's it going, Pop?"

"Good, good." He sat on the stool behind the register sipping what was probably his fourth cup of coffee for the day. "Been a busy mornin'."

"You should have called me."

"Nah. You needed your rest. Besides, I had help."

She wondered if he'd wrangled a neighbor or local teenager to help. "You did? Who?"

Earl gave a nod toward aisle one. "That young fellow of yours."

"Of mine?" Joy turned and her gaze collided with Sam's. Her stomach turned inside out.

Sam knelt beside a boxful of Christmas wrap, unloading the rolls into the bin. His shoulders filled out the blue flannel shirt, making them look as wide and full as the open sky. For some reason he seemed larger, bigger. She felt crowded, as if he was constantly encroaching on her space, even when he was half a room away. He gave her a slanted smile, and a mischievous gleam brightened his eyes to silver.

"B-but...I thought..." She swallowed her statement. She wasn't about to admit she'd been on the lookout for him. When had he returned to the shop? But she knew she couldn't ask that question without giving herself away. Still, she felt as if he was successfully worming his way into her life, and she couldn't yank him out. Jerking her chin, she demanded, "What are you doing here?"

"Helping your dad." He stood, straightening his legs and rising to his full unparalleled height. How did he always make her feel small, vulnerable, defensive? "Are you feeling better?"

"I was." *Until you showed up again.*

Her not-so-subtle jab only made his smile broaden. "I'm glad you slept in. I was worried about you yesterday. But you look better today."

She crossed her arms over the top of her belly. "What do you mean by that?"

Out of the corner of her eye, she saw her father

give a slight shake of his head. But he wasn't aiming it at her. He was signaling Sam!

Sam cleared his throat and stepped forward. "I didn't mean anything by it, Joy. Yesterday, you seemed tired. Today, you look…well, refreshed…radiant."

"Definitely got that pregnancy glow," Pop affirmed.

She scowled. Her gaze slid from Sam to her father, who gave a sharp, approving nod this time. What was happening? Had she made a mistake hiding out in her bedroom all morning? Inadvertently leaving these two alone?

Suspicious, she glared at her father, "What's going on here?"

"Not a thing, sugar. You getting hungry? I am. I could sure use a sandwich or something. Wanna close up for an hour and let's go—"

"I never close for lunch," Joy stated, "and you never have, either." Her brow furrowed. "Has your fever gone back up?"

"I'm not sick. Just hungry. Tired of all that soup you've been feeding me. A man needs something substantial, right, Sam?"

She frowned. "Want me to make you a sandwich?"

"Sure. Let's have a picnic." Pop had undoubtedly lost his mind. "Maybe Sam could help you—"

"I don't need his help, thank you." Then she knew what was going on between these two men. She shot Sam a look that said to keep his distance.

"I should be moseying on," Sam said. "I need to pick up Lacey from school, anyway."

That was a relief.

"Well," she said, trying to sound gracious in spite of her earlier tone, "we're sorry you can't join us." Pleased at the outcome, she smiled to herself and mumbled, "Maybe some other time."

That's enough, Joy. Don't go overboard!

Sam picked up the empty box. "I'll just put this in the back storeroom for you."

"Don't worry about it. I can get it later—"

"You don't need to be lifting anything more than a snowflake." He walked past her and headed toward the back.

She felt her father staring at her with that frown that could shrivel any rebellion. But she kept her eye on Sam. After he'd deposited the box, he returned and grabbed his Stetson from behind the front counter.

"Thanks, Sam." Pop lifted his coffee mug in salute. "You were a mighty fine help today. Come on by tomorrow if you can spare the time."

"Will do." He headed toward the front door, then paused and turned back, looking directly at Joy. "I hear there's a Christmas festival on Saturday night."

Oh, no! She braced herself for the inevitable, and her mind churned with possible excuses.

"There sure is," Pop said.

Sam's gaze remained on her, penetrating her mind, searching her soul. She shifted uncomfortably.

"Can anybody go?" he asked.

"I suppose." But she wouldn't be there this year, even though Charlie had tried to convince her otherwise.

"Good." He slapped his hat on his head and

pulled the narrow brim toward his nose. ''Then how about it?''

Her father sputtered his coffee and shook his head again.

''How about what?'' Her heart jerked out of rhythm.

''How about accompanying me? You said maybe some other time on that picnic.''

''You want to go on a picnic in this weather? It's ten below.''

''I didn't mean a real picnic. I meant share a meal.''

She shook her head, trying to find the words to turn him down when a tiny, rebellious part of her wanted to agree. ''You don't need a date to attend the festival.''

''I don't want any date. I want you.''

The intensity in his gaze made her heart stop momentarily. Her skin tightened. Her jaw started to drop until she caught it and snapped her mouth closed. If only she could believe him. If only he wanted her...not her baby...not anything else...just her. Slowly, she shook herself out of the stupor and back to reality. For some reason, she couldn't turn him down flat. She blamed it on Pop's presence, and his stern disapproving look.

''What about Lacey?'' she asked, throwing up another barrier between them.

''Oh, I'll keep her!'' her father chimed in.

''Pop—''

''It'll be preparation for when you have that baby. Except it'll be easier. No diapers.'' Pop chuckled to himself.

"Good," Sam said, "then it's settled. I'll pick you up around six."

Exasperated and exhausted from battling both of them, Joy said, "The festival doesn't begin until eight."

Opening the door, he gave her a friendly wink. "Then that'll give us plenty of time."

A shiver of anticipation, which quickly turned to concern, rippled down her spine. "For what?"

"To eat." Lowering his voice, he whispered so only she could hear, "Or did you have something else in mind?"

"THAT MAN!" JOY STORMED UP the stairs to their living quarters. "He's going to drive me crazy one of these days."

Chuckling, Pop followed behind. "Sounds like you're serious about him."

"I'm not! He's a mistake…a bad mistake that I made. A mistake that I have to remember every time I look at him."

"And every time you try to tie your shoes." He looked pointedly at her rounded stomach.

She placed a protective hand over her baby. "No. Never."

Pop gave her a sympathetic smile. "What's the big deal about going out with him, anyway?"

"What's the big deal?" She felt her blood pressure rising as she thought of the very big deal it would be to spend time alone with Sam. He tilted her world off center. He flustered her. He made her want… "I'll tell you what the big deal is. He wants to marry me."

"So?"

She yanked open the refrigerator door and pulled out the leftover roast they'd had the other night, along with a loaf of sourdough bread and sandwich fixings. "Pop, I know this is hard for you to understand."

"Try me. I'm not as dense as you like to think."

Grabbing a knife she carved the roast beef. "He wants to marry me for the baby."

"And this is a problem? As opposed to a man who didn't want to marry you for the baby's sake? A man who could care less? A man who felt no responsibility at all?"

She slapped the sandwiches together. Hot, angry tears burned the backs of her eyes. "He doesn't care about *me*. I know that sounds selfish, but I always imagined I'd have a marriage like you and Mom had."

She felt a gentle hand on her back. Trying not to give in to the emotions flooding her soul, she cut her father's sandwich in two and placed it on a plate. "Here." She turned away before he could see her tears. "What would you like to drink?"

"Whatever you're having."

"Milk?"

"That's fine." He sat at the round kitchen table where they'd shared a lifetime of meals together, with and without her mother. "Joy, sugar, even our marriage wasn't perfect."

Her head snapped in his direction. "What do you mean? What are you saying?"

"Nothing. We weren't some fairy-tale couple. We were flesh and blood. We loved each other deeply.

But it wasn't a perfect marriage. There isn't such a thing. Every couple has their problems."

"But—"

"I know it seemed ideal to you, sugar. But you still have a child's idealized perspective about your parents' relationship. If your mother had lived—" his voice broke "—well, I think you would have eventually gone through what most kids do. You would have seen our relationship for what it was— two people loving each other and trying their best to make it work.

"I adored your mother. And she loved me. That's all that matters now. But I hate to think we gave you a picture so perfect that nothing could ever live up to it."

She took a step toward him, her heart softening, turning to mush. "Pop—"

He raised his hand to silence her. "Your perspective about Sam is blurred also."

Her spine stiffened with resentment.

"Maybe you should give him a chance. He is the baby's father. And one way or another, you're going to have to learn to deal with him. Whether it's in marriage or simply in shared custody."

That thought sent shivers down her spine. "Shared custody?"

"Your child deserves a chance to get to know both parents. Don't warp her outlook on life by denying her what your mother's death denied you."

His words struck a raw nerve in Joy. Is that what she would be doing? She smoothed her hand down the side of her belly, felt a decisive kick, and her stomach rippled with the baby's movement. She wanted what was best for her baby. Was she putting herself first rather than the child?

"He's not a bad guy, Joy."

"How do you know?" She sat at the table opposite her father, heard the familiar squeak of the chair hinges that dated back to her parents' early married days. "How do you know anything about him?"

"I've learned to read people over the years. And I can tell this is a good egg."

"I'm not buying produce, Pop. What if I want to marry Charlie?"

He bit into his sandwich. "You don't. He's not your type. But Sam...well, he's a good match for you."

"Is he the type of man you would have chosen for me?"

Pop scratched his beard and washed down his bite with a sip of milk. "I can't say. You'll understand someday soon when you're a parent. You don't think anyone is good enough for your baby. But then you know that they're going to choose someone, and you want that someone to make your baby happy."

"And you think Sam could make me happy? Even though he doesn't love me?"

"I think you should give him a chance. It's just dinner and a dance! I'm not asking you to elope on Saturday."

She leaned on the kitchen table for support. She hadn't expected her father to turn on her and take Sam's side. Feeling slightly betrayed, she tried to look at the situation objectively. Pop was only trying to help, only looking out for her best interests. But was Sam the best for her?

She didn't know. But she trusted Pop's instincts.

"Maybe you're right. I do have to get used to Sam being around. I don't think he's leaving." She jerked her chin and met her father's kind gaze. "But I'm not marrying him."

Chapter Ten

Courting. Sam hadn't courted anyone in years. Not since he'd dated his ex-wife. And look where that had gotten him!

He'd never courted or really dated Joy. When he'd met her, there had been instant mutual chemistry. More like an explosion, fusing them together. He hadn't tried to impress her, nor had he been nervous like he usually was on first dates; instead he'd felt a unique bond with her. She'd been easy to talk to, easy to share the burden of that painfully lonely night, easy to fall in love with.

No. It hadn't been love. It had been lust. Hadn't it?

It had been Lacey's fifth birthday. And he'd been hundreds of miles away from his daughter. It had almost killed him.

Joy had seemed to understand his sorrow, his grief. She'd soothed the heartbreaking misery of separation he was feeling from his family and somehow made him feel like he was a good father in spite of the forced absence in his daughter's life. At least he'd *wanted* to be with Lacey. At least he could call her, send her a present. Which he'd already done.

He hadn't known then that on some level Joy had been identifying with his daughter because of her own absentee mother—one who couldn't write or call or even say "I love you."

From the start she'd been different from any other woman he'd ever known. He felt as if they were walking through their relationship backward. What should have started as a proper courtship had spiraled out of control, and now he was trying to court the mother of his child.

Tonight, unlike their first night together, he didn't have to worry about Lacey, who was safe and secure with Joy's father. Earl was probably reading stories about the real St. Nicholas and making his daughter grilled cheese sandwiches and tomato soup. Tonight, he could concentrate on Joy, not on erasing his guilt and pain. Tonight, he could show her how romantic he could be, how kind and considerate, how he'd make not just a good father for their baby but a decent husband for her.

But how did he do that?

He'd brought her a small bouquet of hard-to-find flowers when he'd picked her up for their date. He'd opened doors, held her chair as she sat down at the restaurant and encouraged her to order anything she wanted regardless of the price or calories. But nothing he did broke through the shell she'd placed around her heart. She seemed distant, aloof, cool toward his attention. That made him antsy, nervous, like a cowboy about to be thrown off his mount. What was he doing wrong now?

"Can I get you anything?" he asked. "More bread? More water? An appetizer?"

For the first time that evening a smile lifted the corner of her tempting mouth. "You sound more like the waiter than my date...I mean, escort...uh...that's not what I meant."

He grinned and sidestepped telling her he considered this a real date. No need to get on her bad side. Maybe she was as nervous as he was. "Did I tell you how beautiful you look tonight?"

She dipped her chin and readjusted her napkin in her disappearing lap. "More like a dressed-up watermelon, I'd say."

"Well, at least you're playing your part right."

She lifted her gaze to meet his. "What do you mean?"

"Most pregnant women, at least the ones I've been around, feel that way. Never able to see how beautiful they really are. I guess you're comparing yourself to the image you have of yourself before you became pregnant."

"When did you become a psychiatrist?"

He laughed as the awkwardness between them began to evaporate. "When I became a parent. Believe me, it changes your perspective on a lot of things, makes you more observant, more tolerant."

She flattened her lips into a thin line. "Hmm."

"What's wrong?" What had he said this time?

"You're not the only one lately who's been telling me my perspective is all wrong."

"I didn't mean to insult you or anything." Concern tightened his shoulders. He seemed to be doing everything wrong. Maybe he should keep his mouth shut.

"It's not you. It's…" She twirled the fork beside her plate idly. "Oh, it doesn't matter."

He reached across the table and stilled her hand beneath the weight of his. Her skin felt warm, electrifying. Tiny sparks erupted down his spine. An urge to kiss her seemed overwhelming, but he knew that would be the wrong move and resisted. "It matters to me."

She shrugged, sliding her hand out from beneath his grasp. He took her silent signal as a clue and leaned back into his chair, giving her space.

"Pop and I were talking the other day about marriage." She averted her gaze, and he felt a sharp jab in the gut.

Marriage, he wondered, or him? Had the conversation been before or after her father had agreed to help with this endeavor to marry Joy? Uncertainty gave him a chill. He felt as if he were about to climb on the back of an unfamiliar bull without knowing its stats or the way it liked to spin.

"And?" he prompted.

"He thinks I have a warped perspective of my folks' marriage."

"Don't we all?" He chuckled at her startled look. "Look, Joy, it's hard for kids to see their parents as teenagers or young adults falling in love, sharing that first kiss…."

Boy, did he remember the first kiss he'd shared with Joy. Just the memory made his insides tighten with need. He knew a reenactment might send him over the edge. Already his pulse was throbbing at the mere thought of tasting her, feeling the texture of her velvety lips against his, having her open to him, give to him completely.

"Haven't you heard kids say that their folks never 'did it'?" he asked, noticing her cheeks flare pink. "It's too bizarre for most kids to envision."

"But I believed my parents were the exception. I knew they loved each other. I saw them kiss and snuggle and love boldly, unconditionally."

"Now you think they didn't?" he asked, wondering what her father had said to upset her.

"I don't know. Pop said that I'd idealized their marriage. That they were two ordinary people trying to make it work. But that doesn't coincide with what I remember."

"Sure it doesn't. You weren't with them during their private moments. You probably don't remember or didn't see them argue or disagree. Even if they did, it doesn't mean they didn't love each other. No marriage is perfect, because it's made up of two imperfect people. Maybe your memory is skewed because of your mother's death."

Just as he knew his was because of his mother's abandonment. But he also knew the dark reality of his own failed marriage.

"The fact is," he said, "your father remembers the good and bad. You still have a child's eye view of your mother. But together your parents lived the reality, the day in and day out of learning to compromise. That's what marriage is, you know."

"Compromise? I thought it was love and commitment."

"Sure, but it takes compromise to make it work.

The husband squeezes the tube of toothpaste from the bottom, the wife from the middle. He leaves damp towels on the floor. She picks them up. He takes out the garbage. She hires a maid.''

"Now, that kind of compromise I like." She gave him a wry grin.

Desire smacked him right between the eyes. His skin tingled with need. His gut burned for her. Could he reach a compromise with Joy?

He realized at that moment that he wanted to marry her more than just to form a family, more than to protect his unborn child. He wanted Joy. Plain and simple...or rather, intricate and complicated.

"So is that what your wife did? She squeezed from the middle, picked up after you and hired a maid?"

"I was never home often enough for her to have to pick up after me. We had separate tubes of toothpaste. But she did hire a maid and yard man and anything else she thought she deserved or couldn't live without."

"So what was the compromise you couldn't agree on?" she asked, leaning forward as if truly interested.

"I had to make enough money to pay for it all. That's what kept me on the road constantly. I couldn't afford to get hurt. I couldn't afford to miss a rodeo. I couldn't afford to take time off to be with my family."

"Doesn't sound like much of a compromise." Her eyes softened as she looked at him. "Are you sure you didn't *want* to be on the road constantly?"

He didn't want her judgment, only her understanding, but her tone of voice sounded more accusing. "I wanted to be with my family. Don't you remember the night we met?"

"Yes, I remember." Her gaze turned solemn. "I'm sorry, Sam. I know you better than that."

He gave an uncomfortable shrug. "You're right, it wasn't much of a compromise, at least on her part. That's why it didn't work. All those nights alone...well, she got bored."

Joy's eyes widened.

He nodded in answer to her silent question. "She found somebody who could make as much as I was making or more to keep her in the style of living she required and who could be home every night. By the time I found out, it was too late."

"Oh, Sam...I'm sorry." This time she reached across the table and touched his hand lightly. It sent a surge of untamed heat through him.

He clenched his hand as he remembered why he didn't want to give Joy his heart. He could still feel the harsh pain, the severe agony of losing everything he'd worked so hard to maintain, especially Lacey.

"I would have fought for our marriage. I would have tried to make it work. I would have found a new career. I would have done anything to keep our family together. But you can't hold someone who wants her freedom." Like his mother. Like his ex. "And once I'd lost her, then I realized I'd really been doing it all for Lacey.

"In trying to please my ex-wife, I'd missed out on the most important things in life—seeing Lacey born, watching her take her first steps, hiding money under her pillow when she loses her first tooth. I swore to myself that someday, somehow I'd have her back in my life.''

''How did you get custody?'' Joy leaned back in her chair.

He paused while the waiter placed their salads in front of them, then he said, ''It was inevitable. My ex-wife was more interested in appearances than meeting Lacey's needs. Her new husband wasn't interested in caring for a stepdaughter. He wanted his own child. So when she got pregnant, it was time for Lacey to go live with her daddy. I quit the rodeo the next day.''

''And now you're trying to make up to Lacey for all the times you missed.''

''I'll never be able to do that. But, yes, I do feel guilty for not giving her a real family. And I am trying to make new memories for her, wonderful memories that she can carry throughout her life that will remind her how much I loved her. I know the pain that comes from a broken home. I never wanted that for Lacey. And I don't want that for our child.''

A shadow crossed Joy's face, darkening her eyes. ''Our child isn't coming from a broken home. You can't break what was never in place.''

''She'll know what she's missing. Especially when she gets in school and sees her friends who have both a mama and daddy at home every night.''

Joy jabbed her fork into the shredded lettuce. ''You can't make a home out of a business arrangement. Where would the compromise you talked about come from then? Would it always be a bargaining chip?'' She shook her head. ''It can't work unless there's a partnership of love, commitment and trust. Without that, it wouldn't last, anyway.''

Trust. That word rang in his head. How could he trust Joy? She'd walked out of his life, just like his mother, just like his ex. He'd have never known about their baby if he hadn't accidentally stumbled into her again. Joy hadn't even told him she was pregnant, much less her own identity, when they'd met here in Jingle. He'd had to learn about his baby through a stranger! Anger clenched his gut into a restrictive knot. That lack of trust would keep him from ever giving her his heart.

''I disagree.'' Simply because he believed there was more here than a business arrangement between them. There'd always been more. That's what he'd been afraid of. That's what unnerved him now. And that's what could be his undoing.

''Determination and commitment can keep a marriage together,'' he continued. ''That is, if we can keep selfishness out. That's why my marriage ended. But I'm willing to take the chance again, because I believe marriage is the best possible solution for both of us now.''

JOY DABBED HER MOUTH with her napkin and pushed the last few bites of salad to the side of her plate. ''Sam, I understand your bitterness toward women, your hesitancy to love and trust. But do you really think you can make a marriage based on something less work?''

''I know I have to try. Not for me. But for our baby.''

Her heart yearned for more, ached for him to open

his heart. And until he could, she'd keep hers tightly locked away.

"Don't you think this discussion has become too serious for shish kebabs and steak?" he asked as the waiter brought their main courses.

She nodded with relief, more than ready to change subjects. "Agreed."

He carved into his steak. "So tell me about this festival."

"It's the usual. Drinking, music, dancing, booths where locals can sell their wares."

"Sounds like fun."

"I suppose."

"You don't want to go?" His brow scrunched into a frown.

"Sure, we can go. I didn't realize I'd be so tired after working in the store all day."

"I should have come by to help."

She leaned her forearm against the table's edge and met his gaze squarely. "Sam, I'm not your responsibility. You don't have to chip in and help at the shop. You have Lacey to take care of and your ranch to run."

She had no one. No one to watch out after her. Oh, there was Pop. But she wanted...yearned for more. And Sam was the only likely candidate who could satisfy her needs. But his focus was the baby...not her. Reality carved a piece out of her heart.

Shoving away her disappointment and pain, she shifted her own focus. "What did Lacey have you doing today?"

"Putting lights up around the house. I stood on

the ladder and she pointed out what I was doing wrong.''

Joy smiled. ''Preparation for womanhood.''

He nodded.

They ate the rest of the meal mostly in silence with a few comments thrown in like salt and pepper to keep things lively. Joy had a hard time concentrating on anything but Sam. His views of marriage spun around her head. The strength and passion he'd demonstrated in wanting to save his marriage and his willingness to do whatever it took to make it work had moved her. If only he'd feel that way toward her. If only his determination to marry her was grounded in love. If only he'd be willing to put his heart on the line. But she knew this was another warped fantasy that could never come true.

Still, she reasoned, he was trying to reach a compromise with her. He'd acted like the perfect gentleman all evening. He seemed genuinely interested in her. But that didn't equal love. Which definitely didn't add up to marriage.

''Joy,'' he said, interrupting her thoughts, ''I know you're tired, so why don't we call it an evening?''

Disappointment shifted inside her when she should be relieved and delighted to go home early. But she wasn't. Was he bored? Her confidence slipped another notch.

''Whatever you want,'' she said, feeling her heart constrict.

He nodded, paid the check, then escorted her to the door. He helped her on with her wool coat. As she buttoned it up and pulled on her gloves, he stepped out into the dark cold.

When she caught up with him, she turned toward home, dipping her head against the brisk wind. Bitter disappointment whipped through her. The evening would end on a flat, indecisive note. Hadn't he sensed the same feelings, the same urges, the same desires she had?

How could he? She was, after all, big and pregnant. What man would find her sexy and irresistible at this awkward stage?

He caught her elbow in his grasp and turned her back toward him. "I don't think you should walk all the way home."

"But that's how we got here. It's not far. Just a few blocks."

"Not when there's a horse-drawn sleigh ready to do all the work for us." He glanced toward the black sleigh and bay gelding at the edge of the street.

His gesture touched her. Tears filled her eyes.

"Come on, it's cold out here." Sam helped her across the icy sidewalk and into the sleigh.

His hands were sure and swift but left indelible prints on her body. Suddenly she felt alive and vibrant. Then he climbed aboard with her and pulled a thick wool blanket over them, tucking it in at the sides, binding them together in a palpable heat. Her breath snagged on raw emotions, and she looked to Sam, unsure what to expect from him next.

He gave a nod to Mr. Dewberry, who'd been driving tourists and passengers through the ice-coated streets of Jingle for more than thirty years. With a click of his tongue, he urged the horse into action.

The sleigh started with a jarring motion then glided over the streets. Joy fell back against the leather seat and instantly realized Sam had slipped his arm around her shoulders, warming her from the inside out.

"Are you warm enough?" he asked, his breath heating her ear, melting her insides.

She nodded and clasped her hands in her lap.

"Isn't this better than walking?"

Unable to form words in her tight throat, she nodded again.

"If you feel up to it, we'll take a little tour of the town. I know it's all familiar to you. You've probably ridden this sleigh hundreds of times, but…"

"No, I haven't. Not once."

"Never?"

She shook her head, feeling the magnetic pull of his silvery gaze draw her closer to him. She knew she should resist the tug of attraction, but where Sam was concerned she'd realized she was weak.

"Then it'll be our first time together." His gaze turned molten. He pulled her close against his side, his hand moving along her arm, lulling her into a wild, intoxicating dream.

She tried to remember that he had an ulterior motive. He wanted to talk her into marrying him. Maybe he was willing to do whatever it cost to reach that goal, just like he'd been willing to do anything to save his marriage. But her resistance slipped. He seemed to be able to find the cracks in her control until she felt as if she was crumbling, falling for him all over again.

Maybe if she filled the space between them with

talk, she could ignore her fatal attraction to him. Maybe he'd say something to remind her of why she should resist him. Because right now, she wanted to lift her face and let him kiss her from now into next week. But for the life of her, she couldn't think of anything to say, anything to talk about, anything to dull the sparks igniting between them.

"What are you thinking?" he asked, his voice low, warm, husky.

"Me? Um, nothing. Nothing at all." Her nerves crashed like cymbals. "What about you?"

"I was thinking about your family shop. How it's really given you a solid foundation, a history, a place to call home."

"And you never had that, did you?"

He nodded. "What was it like?"

She sighed and leaned into his comforting warmth. Finally something simple and heartwarming to concentrate on. Anything besides Sam!

"As a child it was wonderful. Lively and warm. All my friends wanted to come by the shop after school. My parents were considered 'cool.'

"Then my mom died. And I clung to the store like a lifeline." Those old choking emotions churned inside her. "The shop sustained me, reminded me of my mother, made me feel less lonely.

"But then," she said, her voice faltering, "I began to resent it."

"How come?"

"I felt like I was trapped here. I hadn't really had my own life. I'd taken over my mother's. I'd taken care of Pop, helped him out, kept the house up. At the time I hadn't minded. But then, well, a few months ago, I turned twenty-nine.''

"Ah," he said, as if from experience, "worried about getting old, life passing you by, turning thirty?''

"No." Her throat burned with unshed emotions. She hadn't told anyone of her feelings. Those feelings that had made her flee, taken her to Denver for an extended vacation and hurled her right into Sam. "You see, my mother died when she was twenty-nine. It started me thinking about... She'd accomplished so much with her life. She'd found a man to love. She'd had a child. She'd started a successful business.''

"And you were wondering what you'd done with your twenty-nine years? Other than take over for her?''

"Something like that." She plucked at a loose thread on the blanket covering her rounded belly.

Seven months ago her life had been unraveling thread by thread. Until she'd met Sam. Making love to him had set her back on the right course, shown her what she'd truly wanted in life. Yes, she'd almost instantaneously fallen in love with him. But she'd wanted more than a one-night stand, more than a traveling man. She'd wanted a home, permanence. She'd wanted the kind of love her parents had.

"That's actually what led me to Denver and made it so easy for me to fall into bed with you." Her pulse jumped erratically. She'd said too much, gone too far. But how could she take her words back?

He lifted her chin and stared down at her. His

gaze was full of understanding. But without regret. "We were both hurting then. It was our way of healing, of filling the missing part of our lives."

"Yes, but..."

"No more buts," he said. "Let's not look back anymore. Let's look forward."

And he kissed her.

Chapter Eleven

Sam's mouth slanted across hers. He nipped and tugged playfully, urging Joy to open to him, to meet him halfway, to relive that fantasy night they'd shared seven months ago.

Beneath the onslaught of his kiss, it was far too easy to forget her reasons to resist him. He'd always made her feel more alive than she'd ever felt. She wanted to go on feeling as if every nerve, every cell vibrated with newness. Only Sam made her feel vibrant and rejuvenated, desired and needed.

Was that enough to base a marriage on? Should she trust her instincts? Or run? After all, relying on her intuition about Sam had made her reckless, careless. But the real question that cut straight to her heart was could she trust him?

He cupped her chin tenderly, smoothing his thumb along her jawline, causing tiny ripples inside her belly. Her breasts grew taut with the need to lean into him, to feel his hands touch her, to be intimately close to him once again. Every inch of her remembered the feel of him against her, his erotic touch, his tempting kisses.

He made her want to forget everything she'd ever wanted—true love, which would lead to a rock-solid and romantic marriage. With aching awareness, she remembered him loving her from head to toe, just as he was thoroughly and convincingly kissing her just now. He made her want to throw caution to the wind.

Had she lost her mind…her heart already?

Lifting his head, he looked deep into her eyes. She could feel her heart drumming, pummeling her breastbone, pounding along her pulse points. Somehow her arms had wrapped around his neck, her fingers sifting through the coarse hairs at his nape. The realization stunned her. How had he pulled her reservations right out from under her with one simple kiss?

"Joy," he said, his voice deep and rich as a melted chocolate bar, "will you do me a favor?"

At the moment she'd climb Pike's Peak or face wild grizzly bears. Whatever he wanted. She'd definitely lost her own free will. He held it in the palm of his hand.

"What?" she asked, wondering if he needed exactly what she desired. Would he ask to make love to her again? Would he once more ask her to marry him? Or would he demand it?

She braced herself for the inevitable. He'd already confused her when she was most vulnerable. Now would he convince her marrying him was the right thing to do for them, for her, for their baby?

With him holding her close and mesmerizing her with his magnetic gaze, she couldn't remember the reasons she'd laid out for not marrying him. How much longer could she resist when her body wanted to foolishly fall back into bed with him and her heart wanted to recklessly tumble into marriage?

"Would you come out to the ranch tomorrow?" he asked.

Dazed and confused, she felt the hypnotic effect he'd had on her dissipate. She moved her hands to his shoulders, preparing to push away from him. Did he want to trap her into a marriage? Had he already spoken to the justice of the peace? Or did he want to make love to her deep into the night? What was he planning?

Her nerves twisting with uncertainty, she asked, "For?"

"To help us make Christmas cookies." He gave her a tantalizing smile that knocked her for another loop.

She shook loose the last of the cobwebs ensnaring her thoughts. "Excuse me?"

"You know, those cutout sugar cookies with icing and colored sugar decorating them. I haven't got a clue how to make them. I thought you might know. That you'd be willing to help us."

Us. Sam and Lacey. Would there ever be just Sam and Joy? Probably not. It was probably for the best, anyway. She inhaled, her breath snagging on the ragged edges of disappointment.

Somehow her emotions rose on a crest of resignation. His question endeared her even more to him. Pop had been right. At least he wasn't running out on her, deserting her, abandoning her. Sam was honorable. He wasn't trying to trick her. He was in a difficult situation, trying to make the best of it, trying to do the right thing. How could she blame him for that? She realized then that Sam had become as irresistible as pickles and hot fudge dribbled over hazelnut ice cream.

"Yes," she said, around a sudden hard lump in her throat, "I'll come."

"Good. I'll pick you up around two." He kissed the corner of her mouth, sending a series of tingles down her spine.

She could imagine him bringing her home after making Christmas cookies, kissing her again. What would she do? How could she resist? She might not be able to control herself next time. She might be the one to make a reckless offer rather than waiting for him to take the initiative. "You don't have to—"

"Yes, I do. I don't want you driving alone. Not on these winding roads with foul weather. And I don't like competition."

She was tempted to tell him that Charlie didn't make her feel the way he did. Charlie wasn't his competition. Tom Cruise wouldn't even be able to make her head turn or her heart veer off the path it had chosen. No one could. But she kept her thoughts and feelings to herself, hidden deep inside her heart—where they belonged.

WHEN SAM WALKED IN the back door the next day, stamping snow and ice bits off his boots, he wasn't sure if he'd stepped out of or into a winter wonderland. He shrugged out of his overcoat and hung it on a peg beside the door and smiled to himself. The floury-white scene in his kitchen was infinitely warmer and more welcoming than the blowing snow and howling wind whipping through his pastures. Could life get better than this?

Only if Joy married him. Only if they formed a real family.

"Hi, Daddy!" Lacey gave him a sugary smile. Smudges of white blotched her face and clothes. "Look what we made!"

She jumped off the stool next to Joy and took him by the hand to the kitchen table where at least a dozen Santa cookies were lined up like toy soldiers. Each had been decorated with dollops of white sugar and coated in red frosting. He'd never be able to look at another Santa the same way, at least not since he'd seen Joy dressed up in her father's getup, with her pregnant belly for padding.

"Looks yummy," he said, thinking more of Joy than the cookies and remembering her eager kiss from last night.

"They are!"

Smiling, he wiped the corner of his daughter's mouth to erase a telltale smear of red frosting.

"How's the cattle?" Joy asked.

He smiled at the patch of flour across her rounded belly. His heart swelled at the sight of her. He had to restrain his urge to put his arms around her, pull her close and plant another kiss on her tempting mouth. "Wanting to come in and warm up next to our fireplace."

"I bet." She rolled out a lump of cookie dough onto the counter.

"When can I go riding again, Daddy?" Lacey asked.

"Not until the weather warms up, darlin'. Too cold out there for you. And me."

"Would you like some hot chocolate or cider to warm you up?" Joy asked.

Looking at her, he was getting plenty warm. He had a better idea of how she could start a blaze inside him.

It amazed him that he seemed to be even more attracted to her now than he had been when they'd first met several months ago. It seemed odd that even with her pregnant belly she was even more beautiful and desirable. "That'd be great. But don't stop what you're doing. I'll fix it. Anybody else want some?"

Lacey went back to the counter and watched Joy rolling out the dough. "Can we stop and have a snack?"

Joy smiled. "If we stop and snack every five minutes then we won't have any cookies left when we're finished."

His daughter gave a sheepish grin and climbed back onto the step stool. "What cookie cutter should we use this time?"

"Your choice." Joy spread out an array of metal and plastic cookie cutters that she'd brought from home. "There's a reindeer, sleigh, star…"

"How about the Christmas tree?"

"Perfect." Joy handed the tree-shaped cutter to Lacey. "Just press it into the dough like we did last time."

"Are we gonna make green icing to go on these?"

"Of course! Unless you want red Christmas trees."

Lacey giggled. "That'd be silly."

Sam grabbed a mug out of a cabinet, filled it with the chocolate mix and poured boiling water over the powder. As he stirred the creamy concoction, he watched Joy and his daughter working together. He could never have envisioned his ex-wife enjoying a day of baking. She'd preferred expensive bakery cookies rather than homemade. Maybe it hadn't been simply good taste, as she'd called it, but plain old laziness, arrogance or even ignorance.

"What can I do?" Sam asked, sipping the hot cocoa.

While helping Lacey peel away the unused dough from the cookie cutouts, Joy said, "You could check the oven and see if the angels are ready for frosting."

Sam peeked into the oven and felt heat warm his face. "How can you be sure?"

"If they're slightly brown around the edges and puffed up across the middle," she said, "then they're done."

"Want me to check, Daddy?"

"No, sugar. I don't want you to get burned."

"But Daddy—"

"It's okay, Lacey." Joy dropped a tender kiss on the top of his daughter's head as if Lacey were her own kid. "That's just your father's way of saying that he loves you."

Now Sam had to figure out a way to tell Joy that he loved her. *No, no, that wasn't right. I don't love*

*her. I appreciate her. I respect her. But love? No
way. I'm not doing that again.*

Still, the thought of losing her, of not having her
in his home, family and bed became a constricting
pain in his chest. He knew he had to convince her
to marry him no matter what the cost.

But could he afford her price—his heart?

"STORM'S GETTING WORSE." Sam stared out the
window at the swirling snowflakes.

"Maybe we should get going then," Joy said, not
wanting to get caught in a blizzard, either on the
road or at Sam's ranch. She folded the damp dish
towel and laid it on the counter next to the clean
dishes she'd finished washing.

"It's too late for that." He frowned. "It's not safe
to travel in this kind of weather."

Her nerves jangled together. "But I can't stay
here."

"Why not? I'm not the big bad wolf, you know."

"I'm not so sure about that," she whispered, casting a glance over her shoulder at Lacey, who sat at
the kitchen table eating a cookie and drinking milk
for dessert after dinner.

"I'm not about to risk your life, the baby's or
Lacey's in trying to get you home. All to do what?
Save your reputation?" He gave a pointed look at
her belly.

Okay, he had a point. Having grown up in Colorado, having lost her mother in a car accident, she
wasn't too keen on setting out on icy roads, either.

"Besides—" he stepped closer to her, crowding

her, making her heart beat wildly ''—I'll be the perfect gentleman.''

Why did she want him to be the exact opposite? Had she lost her mind? ''Pop will be worried.''

''I'm not kidnaping you. We have a phone. You can call. He'll understand. I'll explain it to him if you want.''

She knew Pop would agree with Sam's logic. It was the sensible thing to do. After all, Lacey would be here, sort of acting like a chaperone. A five-year-old chaperone. Oh, dear! ''But—''

''What are you worried about?'' He crossed his arms over his broad chest. The seams of his shirt stretched taut over his muscular shoulders. Staring down at her, he seemed as cross as a grizzly having been woken from his winter nap.

What was she worried about? Sam! He worried her. He made her knees tremble, her heart flutter. Just one look or one touch could melt her resolve to keep her distance from him. One kiss could cause an avalanche. And one more night of passion could…

Oh, Lord! She was knee-deep in trouble. Suddenly staying in the same house with Sam seemed more reckless than braving the snowstorm outside.

But she couldn't let him see how he affected her. She couldn't let him glimpse the way he tossed her emotions around like a flimsy snowflake in a gale. Crossing her arms over her chest, she resolved to maintain that distance at all costs. She had to keep him from seeing how much she wanted him and wanted to stay…all night…every night. ''Do you have a spare bedroom?''

He grinned, making a dimple pinch one of his taut cheeks and her pulse skitter helplessly. "Nicer than the best bed-and-breakfast in town. I'll make up the bed myself." His voice dipped low and seemed to trail along her nerve endings like a long, slow caress. "I'll even serve you breakfast in bed if you'd like."

She'd like that too much. It would be decadent. And way too tempting to resist. She glanced out the window, searching for an excuse, a way to flee, but at the same time wanting to stay in this warm, cozy house with Sam. "Surely the storm will be over by then and I can eat breakfast at home."

"Whatever you want." He leaned closer, his warm breath fanning her cheek. "Don't worry, Joy. You'll be safe here with me."

"Is that your word as a Boy Scout?"

He shook his head slowly, gravely. "Never was one." His heated gaze ignited a blaze inside her. "But it's my word as a man."

And she'd have to take it or leave it.

"AND SANTA CALLED happy Christmas to all and to all a good-night." Sam closed *'Twas the Night Before Christmas*. "And that's good-night for you, young lady."

"But, Daddy, I'm not tired."

"Too much sugar," Joy said, folding the top of Lacey's blanket back. She could see the energy shining in the girl's eyes. She could have told Sam his daughter was too wired to settle down, but it wasn't her place.

"Too much excitement," Sam added.

"You're no fun." Lacey rolled out her bottom lip.

"I know," Sam said, unaffected by his child's outburst.

"You don't let me do anything. Mother would let me—"

Sam snapped off the light and a pale pink night-light clicked on automatically. He swaggered toward the bed like John Wayne, twirled the desk chair around on one leg, then mounted it like an obedient steed. "Look here, young lady. While you're in my town, you're gonna have to follow my rules. And I said lights out at nine."

Lacey hid a smile beneath the edge of her covers.

"Now, be a lady and thank Miss Joy for coming all the way out here to help us make Christmas cookies."

Shyly, his daughter glanced at Joy. "Thanks."

"You're welcome."

"Now, give your mean ol' pa a kiss." Sam leaned forward, and Lacey wrapped her arms around his neck.

Feeling her chest constrict with emotions she didn't want to analyze, Joy turned away. She moved quietly toward the door. "G'night."

"Are you gonna be here in the morning?" Lacey asked.

"For a little while. Until your father can drive me back to town."

"Good!" Her eyes shone like Christmas lights. "Can we have cookies for breakfast?"

Sam groaned and rolled his eyes. "I've created a monster."

Joy laughed. "How about if I fix my famous pancakes?"

"What kind?" Lacey bounced in bed. "Blueberries? Bananas?"

"Chocolate chip?" Sam asked, almost as eager as his daughter.

Smiling to herself, Joy shook her head. "You'll have to wait and see." She met Sam's tired gaze. She wondered how she would feel in a few months as she put her infant to bed. Would she be exhausted, frustrated, frazzled? Or as calm and cool as Sam?

The hardest question to answer was whether she'd be wishing she had Sam's help and support. Oh, dear! "G'night."

"I'll be down in a minute," Sam called over his shoulder.

Walking down the stairs, she knew many battles lay ahead of her as she faced parenthood alone. She should probably stay and help Sam calm Lacey down and get her to sleep, but she didn't want to give him any ideas about how they could make a good team or a perfect family. Actually, she didn't want to prove anything to herself. He had to do this himself. Just as she'd have to put her own baby to bed.

SAM KNELT near the fireplace and jabbed the logs with a long poker, making them spew sparks into the chimney. His thoughts were as dark as the ashes along the bottom of the grate. Having Joy help him put his daughter to bed had shown him how it could be between them with their own daughter. And what it would *really* be like if he had his way. He simply had to convince her to marry him.

He couldn't let her put his baby to bed every night without him. He wanted to read bedtime stories, hear prayers, hand out more cups of water. He wanted to turn off the lamp, watch his child in the waning light, listen to the deep, rhythmic breathing of sleep.

But how the heck was he going to change Joy's mind? Or maybe it was her heart he had to convince. Suddenly a bell rang in his head, like a signal...or alarm.

"Lacey enjoyed herself today." He turned toward Joy, who sat on the overstuffed couch, her arms crossed over her chest, her legs tucked beneath her. "Thank you."

"You're welcome. She's welcome. Maybe I should be thanking you. I had fun, too."

Moving toward her, he tried to gauge whether he should sit on the couch with her or aim for the leather recliner nearby. "She didn't want to go to bed tonight. She thought she might miss out on something."

"What?" Joy stiffened, her eyes widening as if she'd been caught with her hand in the cookie jar. "We're not doing anything."

Or maybe she'd been *thinking* of doing something with him. Maybe that's why she looked guilty. Or incredibly innocent. He couldn't decide which. Testing the waters, he eased onto the couch, being sure to leave a wide expanse between them. He wouldn't crowd her or push her into anything. But he wanted to be close to her. It had been torture keeping his distance all day, going to the barn to feed the cattle when he'd only wanted to stay and watch her move through his kitchen as if she belonged there. He could have sat for hours and simply watched her smile.

"Relax," he said, not sure if he was coaching Joy or himself. "I'm not about to pounce on you." That was a message meant for only him. If she wanted to pounce on him, he certainly wouldn't mind.

"I am relaxed." Her hands tightened around her elbows, her knuckles turning as white as the frost collecting on the windows.

He chuckled, releasing the tension in his own body. He tried not to think about the fact that he was alone with Joy. He tried to remember that his daughter, his young, impressionable daughter was upstairs. "You look as relaxed as a long-tailed cat in a room full of rockers."

She offered a reluctant smile. "How did you get Lacey to calm down and go to bed finally?"

"I used the oldest tool known to parents."

Interested, Joy raised her eyebrows.

"I simply said Santa wouldn't bring what she wanted for Christmas unless she was extra good these days. And that meant going to bed on time."

Joy's smile widened, electrifying him. Until the reality of his words to his daughter struck him like lightning. His smile vanished like the sun over the peak of a mountain.

"What's wrong?"

"Santa might not bring what she wants, anyway."

A crease formed between Joy's feathery brows and she leaned slightly toward him, as if she wanted to touch him but didn't dare. "Why do you say that?"

He felt her probing gaze studying, watching, measuring. Was she wondering what kind of a father he really was? What kind of a father he'd make to their child? His hopes at ever changing her mind plummeted. "I don't know what she wants."

Just like he didn't know what Joy wanted. He'd never been good with women. Never had much of a chance learning about them since his mother hadn't stuck around for long. And his first wife had sent him on the road, preferring the house and often the bed to herself. So he'd been a failure as a husband. And now as a father. Why would Joy want to marry him?

"She won't tell me."

"Oh. Is that all?"

"Is that all? What else is there? How else am I supposed to find out?" Suddenly he knew the answer. "She told you a Christmas tree. But she told your dad something else the other day when we were in the shop. Do you think he'd tell me?"

"No way." She dashed his hopes immediately. "Pop doesn't spill the beans on kids. That's why they trust him."

"But—"

"Ever," she emphasized.

"Then how does he know kids will get what they want? Isn't that his job to help their dreams come true?"

She gave a slight shrug. "I don't know. But he's never had a disappointed customer. The kids keep coming back year after year. And they bring their kids. So he must know something. He must be doing something right.''

''Then he must tell the parents. Maybe you just aren't aware—''

She shook her head. ''Never.''

Frustrated, Sam shoved his fingers through his hair. He felt the days between now and Christmas falling like dominoes stacked in a row, crashing in on his hopes and plans for this first holiday with his daughter. ''Then what am I supposed to do?''

''Your best. That's all anyone can ask.''

Not in the least comforted, he sighed and leaned back into the cushions. ''That's not good enough.''

Joy touched his arm, jarring his senses, stirring a raw need inside him. He felt her heat, her tenderness, her concern, right down to his toes. His nerve endings sizzled and popped like the fire crackling in the hearth.

''You're a wonderful father, Sam.'' Sincerity made her eyes a startling blue. ''Don't doubt yourself for a minute. Lacey adores you. And it's obvious that you adore her. That's all that counts. Especially that your daughter knows and feels your love.''

''But what will I do about her Christmas gift?''

''I don't know. But you'll figure something out. You still have plenty of time.''

''Christmas is right around the corner. What if she wants a pony or a puppy or her mother or something that can't be picked up at the last minute? Or something that's totally impossible?''

''Have you talked to her about it?''

''She said she told Santa and that he was taking care of it.''

''Then relax. Believe me, Pop wouldn't let Lacey have a miserable Christmas. I'm sure it will all work out.''

He felt as sure of his abilities as if he were skating on thin, cracking ice. ''What would you get a little girl Lacey's age?''

She shrugged. ''Depends on the girl. Does she like Barbies? Dolls? Maybe clothes or a good old-fashioned Disney movie.''

He frowned. ''She's got gobs of dolls and stuff. We have enough movies to start a video store. I want to get her something that will make Christmas special, memorable.''

''You're putting too much pressure on yourself. She's going to have a wonderful Christmas no matter what you get her.''

''How do you know?''

''I don't think Lacey wants something only money can buy. I think she wants what's been missing in her life. You. That, not some expensive gift, will make Christmas magical for her.''

''I wish I could be certain.''

''That's one thing about kids. You can never be certain about anything.'' She laid her hand against the side of her belly.

''The baby?''

''Yeah. She really likes to move and groove about this time every night.''

''Can I?'' He reached out his hand.

She grasped it and placed it against the round

firmness of her stomach. He felt a nudge, then a sharp jab. He grinned and met Joy's warm gaze.

"Feels like a buckin' bronco."

She laughed. "A li'l barrel racer, you think?"

"You never know. She might be a chip off her old pop." He smoothed his hand along the curve of her belly and clasped Joy's hand, entwining his fingers with hers. "Would you mind?"

Chapter Twelve

Joy felt Sam's gaze boring into her, burrowing inside her very soul as he waited for her answer.

Did she care if their baby took after Sam? Of course she cared! But not in the way he feared.

Sam's jaw was set rock hard and his lips were compressed into a thin line. What at first glance might seem overbearing or surly to someone else had the opposite impression on her. Joy knew Sam better than she'd thought. There was a vulnerability in his gaze, a tension in the slant of his brow, concern tightening his voice, which spoke volumes. Her answer meant more to him than he cared to admit.

But why? Why should it matter to him what she thought or wanted in their child? Did he care more than she'd imagined or hoped for? His insecurity pulled the rug out from under her. She'd seen Sam as a rough-and-tumble cowboy, bent on his own plan, his own needs. She'd even seen him as a questioning, uncertain father. But never had he seemed apprehensive about her feelings. Could it mean his heart was involved?

"No," she said, her voice soft and gentle. "I

wouldn't mind at all if the baby is like you.'' She touched his brow, smoothed a careless lock of hair away from his eyes. ''I'd like it very much if our baby had her father's eyes. Or your smile. Or compassion.''

The strain in his expression eased. The corner of his mouth quirked into a half grin, making her insides thrum. ''But she has to have her mother's body.''

Taking the chance to break the hypnotic trance he seemed to have on her, she laughed and touched her stomach. ''Not *this* body.''

He ran a finger down the curve of her cheek, the slope of her neck and along her shoulder. ''Yes, this very body.'' His gaze traveled over her intimately, knowingly, making her skin tighten with desire. ''There's nothing more beautiful.''

''Or sexy, right?'' Her voice broke with uncertainty.

''No one else can turn me into knots with a look…or kiss the way you can.''

Her heart pounded. What was he saying?

He leaned closer, until she felt his warm breath caress her cheek. Her nerve endings vibrated with anxiety, quivered with need.

''There're a lot of things I'm unsure of these days, from how to raise Lacey to what to expect with this new baby. But there's one thing I am certain about, Joy.'' His thumb rubbed the bottom edge of her lip and made her tremble.

Oh, God! He was going to kiss her. Right here. In his house. On his couch. And how much farther would it be to his bed?

Did she care?

Yes! She'd fallen recklessly into bed with Sam once. She wasn't about to do it again. Or to fall into matrimony with him. He was not professing love. He was simply saying he wanted her. Isn't that what had put her in this situation? "Uh, Sam—"

"Don't you feel this between us? Can't you—"

"It's getting late." She shifted, grabbing the arm of the couch for leverage. The heels of her shoes slipped on the hardwood floor. Her bottom sank deeper into the cushions of the couch. Dammit! She couldn't get up. She was stuck.

When he touched her, she thought she was a goner. She felt herself drawn to him, her body leaning toward him, anticipating, wanting, needing. He cupped her elbow and gave a gentle push to help her to her awkward and swollen feet.

Disappointment washed through her. Why hadn't he taken advantage of her? Why hadn't he just kissed her? The way she'd wanted…needed him to.

Why would he? What man would find a woman too big to get up from the couch attractive? She bet Sam had never tried to kiss a woman and had her waddle away like an oversize duck. She wanted to bury her head in her hands and sob out of sheer frustration. But she swallowed the hormonal, roller-coaster emotions surging and swelling inside her. Those wicked hormones had to be the reason why she bounced from wanting Sam to pushing him away, from fear to disappointment, from determination to desire.

Good grief, Joy! What's wrong with you?

Hormones. Simply hormones.

"I should turn in," she said, her voice rasping with indecision.

He gave a grim nod. "You need your rest. I'll show you to your room."

"No!" She jerked away from him, feeling as if she'd touched a hot cookie sheet without an oven mitt. "I mean, that's okay. I know the way."

He bracketed her shoulders with his hands and held her captive with his penetrating gaze. "I didn't mean to scare you by wanting you so much. You can trust me. I wouldn't do anything you didn't want me to." He pressed a kiss to her cheek. "I'll see you in the morning. Let me know if you need anything."

Need anything? She needed *him!*

No, she needed her head examined. Or her heart.

Because she felt she was losing this battle every second she stayed near Sam.

THE HOUSE WAS DARK and silent. Too silent. Too still. Quiet snow fell, gathering on the sill outside his bedroom window. Alone in the cocoon of his room, Sam stared up at the ceiling.

Lacey was deep in dreamland. He'd checked on her before turning in. Joy was probably sleeping peacefully in the guest room. He'd resisted looking in on her. He wondered if she'd worn the shirt he'd left for her on the bed or slept in her clothes...or nothing at all.

With thoughts like that, he wouldn't get any rest with her beneath the same roof. Hell, he hadn't had a good night's sleep since she'd entered his life. Not just since he'd moved to Jingle and discovered her hiding beneath her father's Santa suit. But ever since he'd met her in Denver, he hadn't been able to banish her from his thoughts or his dreams.

He lay on the top of his covers, his clothes piled in a heap beside the bed where he'd shucked them. He'd tried a cold shower, but that hadn't cooled the fire burning inside him.

What was wrong with him? No woman had ever affected him so profoundly. No one had ever turned his world so completely upside down. Only Joy...

A clank somewhere in the darkness of the house jerked his attention away from her momentarily. Frowning, he sat upright in bed. Had Lacey gotten up for a drink of water? Was she sick? Or was it Joy? Concern tightened his shoulders. Maybe something was wrong. He doubted she'd come get him or even ask for his help.

Shoving his legs into his jeans, he zipped on his way out the door. He padded his way down the stairs, following the faint sounds drifting through the darkness. A sliver of light shone beneath the kitchen door.

Easing it open without making a sound, he saw Joy standing in front of the stove. Desire flared inside him at the sight of her. She wore his buttondown shirt, the shoulders drooping over hers, the tail skimming the back of her thighs, making her look small and guileless, feminine and sexy. A raw need pulled taut like a lead rope within him.

Her feet were bare, her toes curling toward the coolness of the hardwood floor. He wanted to go to her, wrap his arms around her, kiss her thoroughly and convincingly....

But what would he be convincing her of? That he wanted her? That he needed her? Yes, dammit! Was that such a terrible thing?

Hell, yes. He'd already been as weak and vulnerable as a baby calf this evening. She didn't need him panting after her like some lovesick bull. She needed to see his strength. And he'd use that strength to resist any urges at the moment.

"Caught you," he said.

She sucked in a breath and whirled around to face him. Her hand clasped his shirt closed at the base of her throat. "Wh-what…what are you doing here?"

"I live here."

"You startled me."

"I heard a mouse creeping around. I wanted to make sure it wasn't Lacey sneaking another cookie."

"Nope—" she smiled "—just me." She pulled the teakettle off the burner. "Actually, I was just making some hot chocolate. Would you like some?"

"Couldn't you sleep?" His insides twisted at the anticipation of her answer. What if she said yes? Did that mean she wanted him as much as he wanted her? Had she been thinking of him, imagining them together again? Or was it a pregnancy thing?

Placing her hand just above her hip, she arched her back. "My back's killing me and the baby is treating me like she's the drummer in a rock band."

His hopes dashed, he released his disappointment. What did he expect? She was pregnant. With his child! What did he think, that she wanted to jump his bones? Feeling the awesome responsibility not only for the baby but also for Joy's well-being, since it was his fault she was pregnant, he decided to try to relieve some of her discomfort.

"Hot chocolate won't cure what ails you." He crossed the room and took her by the hand, leading her back into the dark den. The banked fire gave the room a soft, intimate glow.

"What are you doing?" Her voice sounded strained.

He draped a handmade quilt across the rug in front of the fireplace and added several pillows to the makeshift bed. "Come here."

"Sam…"

"I'm not going to hurt you."

She stared at him, her eyes wide.

"You're looking at me like I'm the big bad wolf."

"Aren't you?"

"No. Now, come here."

She took a hesitant step toward him, then a bolder one. "What do you want?"

You. But he resisted stating the obvious. "I'm going to give you one of my world-famous back rubs."

"A back rub?"

"It'll help you sleep a lot better than hot chocolate."

Doubt turned her eyes a misty gray. "The caffeine really isn't good for the baby."

"See? Now, come on, what are you so afraid of?"

She lifted her chin. "I'm not afraid."

"Then lie down and let me work my magic on you."

Her hand touched the slight bulge beneath the shirt he'd leant her. "Haven't you worked enough magic on me?"

He grinned. "I promise to be a gentleman."

PLEASE DON'T. Don't be a gentleman, Joy wanted to shout. But at the same time she wanted to run back into the guest bedroom and bolt the door. Not because she didn't trust Sam. She didn't trust herself.

Love me, Sam. Please love me. Make me believe that what we shared was more than a one-night stand, more than a careless act of two needy people, more than…nothing. Love me truly.

That first and only night together had meant more to her. But she wasn't sure what it had meant to him. She'd convinced herself when she'd left that morning so many months ago that she'd been one in a long string of fillies prancing through the cowboy's life. Now she knew that wasn't true. Maybe, just maybe, that night had meant more to him, too. But how could she be sure?

With the heat of the banked fire warming her, she lay on her side, her head supported by a pillow. The smooth, circular motions he used as he kneaded the tired muscles along her spine both soothed and aroused. Her skin tingled. Her pulse skittered and raced. Her insides turned pliable.

But Sam would never cross the line she'd drawn. His gentleman or cowboy code was stronger than any Boy Scout oath. And it only made her want him…love him more.

Even as his fingers probed and stroked, moving along the column of her spine, stirring elicit feelings inside her, she wanted to pull him down to her and kiss him. Instead, she lay perfectly still, not daring to move and risk the chance that he might stop his slow, unintentional seduction. He massaged her neck and shoulders, taking his time, not missing an inch, drawing out of her a low moan of pleasure.

"Are you comfortable?" he asked, leaning down to whisper in her ear. The soft brush of his breath against her nape made her quiver inside.

"Mmm. Very."

"Tell me if I hurt you."

"You're not."

"If I'm helping or not."

"You are."

"Good."

Slowly, carefully, he moved down to the base of her spine. His fingers moved gingerly, pressing, rubbing, turning her limbs to mush. His movements were efficient, skilled, competent. And erotic.

Nothing he did evoked passion or made her uncomfortable or wary. But her own thoughts and reactions did. She'd crossed that line long ago. And there was no going back. Maybe if they relived that night they'd shared, if they joined intimately, then she could face the truth in Sam and herself. Maybe then she could move on with her life. With or without him.

One of his hands crept over the edge of her belly. He pressed his flat palm to the round side of her stomach. "How's the baby doing?"

"Fine." Gathering her courage, she rolled onto her back. At first she was stunned that Sam had shifted his position. He was no longer sitting behind her but had settled onto his side as well. He urged her to face him until they were only inches apart.

The darkness blanketed them. She felt the warmth of the fire at her back and Sam's heat pulling her toward him. His gaze was dark and glittering like bits of coal. Her heart thudded; her pulse roared in her ears.

"How are you feeling?" he asked, hooking a lock of hair behind her ear. "Better?"

She nodded, unable to find words to convey her feelings.

"I'll keep working on your back if you need me to."

"No, that's okay."

"Do you think you can sleep now?"

Not a chance! "I'm not tired anymore."

He frowned. "But you need your rest."

"I'm okay, Papa Bear."

He grinned. "Feels strange to think of being a daddy again."

Her heart stilled. "Strange good or bad?"

"Definitely good." His hand caressed her stomach and his eyes reflected awe. "I'm looking forward to it. It feels good having you with Lacey and me. Like fate somehow brought us here. So we could be together as a family."

His words tapped into her greatest need and brought tears to her eyes. Her throat constricted with emotions that she couldn't voice. How she wanted to belong here with him, with his daughter, as a family. But could they overcome the doubts and mistrust standing between them?

She knew a part of Sam didn't trust her. After all,

she'd kept the knowledge of her pregnancy from him. She'd told herself he would have been difficult to locate. But she hadn't even tried. She'd also left him, as his ex-wife and mother had. Could she blame him for his doubts?

In order for him to get past his feelings and somehow come to care for her, then she would have to build the bridge between them. It was up to her. Her life, their family and her baby's future lay in her own hands.

"Sam," she said tentatively.

"I know, you don't want to hear that I think of us as a family. You think I'm about to propose again, that I'm just trying to hog-tie you into marriage. But—"

She pressed her fingertips to his lips. "I wasn't going to say that at all."

When she faltered, he covered her hand with his and rested it against his heart. "What were you going to say?"

Taking a ragged breath, she took the plunge. "That it felt right to me, too."

He paused, taking a slow, deliberate breath. "What are you saying, Joy? Are you reconsidering?"

"I'm considering. That's all I know at the moment. Right now, I just want to spend time with you." Her skin burned. "Alone."

"You've got me." He grinned.

A nervous giggle rippled out of her throat. "What I meant was…that I…that we…"

His heated gaze unnerved her. Doubts assailed her. Would he change his mind if he saw all the changes that had occurred to her body? Would he be turned off by a pregnant woman? Would he push her away or leave her in the cold light of morning?

"What do you want, Joy?" he asked, his voice full of patience and understanding.

"You."

"I'm right here."

"I know but...I want more. I want to be... closer."

In the dim light, she saw his eyebrow lift and his eyes glitter. "I made you a promise that I won't break."

She felt the steady pounding of his heart beneath her palm and it reassured her. "What if I do?"

For a long while he remained silent and her nerves began to unravel into tiny threads of doubt. *What have you done, Joy?* Needing to get this over with, so she could run upstairs and hide her embarrassment, she pressed on. "Sam?"

"I'm waiting," he replied, his voice dipping low into a seductive tone, almost a challenge. "It's your move, darlin'."

Feeling awkward and nervous, she smoothed her hand up along his neck, feeling his hot skin burn into her, and cupped his firm jaw. "I don't know what to do."

"Yes, you do. Follow your instincts, Joy. Don't think so much."

She took a deep, shuddering breath and focused on Sam, on what they'd shared together, on what they would share in the future with this baby. How it would all tie together, she wasn't sure, but she had to take this step. So much depended on her strength and determination now.

And she kissed him. At first he was unresponsive, almost cold. She jerked back and blinked. "What's wrong? I thought you wanted me to..."

"Do you really want this, Joy?" Then she felt a trembling in his hand, as if he were using every ounce of restraint to hold back.

No longer having doubts, she answered, "Yes."

"Then prove it."

Chapter Thirteen

With Sam's challenge ringing in her ears, Joy dipped her head again and kissed him, teased him, tempted him until she wasn't sure who was the aggressor anymore. They met halfway, both greedy, both wanting more.

Even as she felt their hearts racing together, each touch, every caress remained slow in a teasing exploration of flesh and response. Gently, he peeled away the shirt covering her, taking one button at a time, uncovering her bit by bit to his warm, appreciative gaze. The coolness in the room made her shiver, but his hands warmed her until she burned with a slow heat radiating from the inside out.

Nervous at his erotic examination, she grasped his shoulders as he buried his face between her breasts, nuzzling, caressing, kissing her nipples until they grew hard with desire. "I've changed a bit since...since..."

"You're beautiful," he murmured, his mouth hot against her skin.

"I'm bigger."

Kissing his way up to her mouth, he whispered, "There's something to be said for size."

She felt his erection pressing against her thigh, and her insides tightened with awareness and need to feel him a part of her again. "Show me."

He explored her rounder body. He paid extra attention to her breasts, fondling her tightening nipples, weighing the soft mounds in his hands. He kissed, stroked, caressed every inch of her until she was clutching, clawing, gripping his back with a raw, aching need.

"Oh, Sam…" She arched her neck and back, needing to feel him inside her.

"Are you okay?" He paused, his body tense.

"I'm fine. Don't stop."

"Is this okay? I mean, for the baby? For you?"

"We're both fine. Sex is okay in pregnancy. The doctor said so."

He rose up on his elbow and stared down at her. "He said you could have sex? That was irresponsible of him, wasn't it?"

She chuckled. "I'm sure he tells all his patients that. He wasn't giving me the green light to go paint the town red or anything."

After a long pause, Sam trailed a finger along her cheek. "I don't want to hurt you."

"You won't." She wrapped her arms around his waist and rubbed her breasts against his chest. "Now, kiss me."

"Yes, ma'am." He dipped his head and made good on his promise.

Lovingly he took pleasure in her body, testing, teasing, eliciting soft moans and fever-pitched pleas.

After he slipped off her panties and removed his jeans, tossing them both beside the hearth, he smoothed his hands along her belly and nestled himself into the center of her until she moaned and writhed against him.

She wondered why she'd ever felt self-conscious about her pregnant body. With each loving touch, each tender kiss, each erotic stroke of his fingers, she sensed his desire and need was as strong as her own. The tide of passion that carried them to a crest overwhelmed her with its emotional intensity. This time their bonding seemed to be on a deeper level, more than two hurting people clinging to each other.

As he joined with her, they became one, reaching for the same goal, searching for the same thing in their life. When her body shuddered in climax, he allowed himself release and collapsed beside her, careful to avoid her stomach with the weight of him but still securing her against his side. She burrowed her face against his shoulder and prayed they would find what they both needed. Together. As one.

THE FIRST TIME they'd made love, Sam had been stunned by the intensity, drained emotionally, overwhelmed and undone by her disappearance. This time, he realized he'd missed out on so much in his marriage. There had never been a true bonding between his ex-wife and him, not like the deep, emotional connection he'd forged with Joy. And he wasn't about to let her get away a second time.

Her soft crying jerked him out of the dazed fog of lovemaking. "What's wrong?" His heart jackknifed. "Are you in pain? Damn! I hurt you."

She shook her head, but her response was muffled against his shoulder.

"Dammit, Joy!" He tempered his voice to keep from waking his daughter upstairs but grasped Joy's shoulders in desperation. "Talk to me. Should I call the doctor?"

"I'm okay, just hormonal."

"What do you mean?"

"I weep at everything these days—sappy commercials, comedies, making love. Romantic, huh?"

"Sweet," he said, erasing a tear from her cheek. Bending low, he sipped the tears from the corners of her mouth, then pressed another kiss to her lips. "Are you sure it's hormones and not something more?"

She shrugged. "It's probably a lot more."

Maybe she really was considering marrying him. He wanted them to be a family, but at the same time new doubts plagued him. Could they make it work? He didn't want to put Lacey or this baby through a divorce. He *had* to be sure before they took their vows.

"I'm here if you want to tell me about it," he said, hoping to glean some understanding from her.

"Can't we simply share this time together?"

"Will talking destroy that? I thought it might bring us closer. If that's possible."

"You felt it, too, then?"

His heart constricted with an odd mixture of fear and hope. "How could I not?"

She sighed and relaxed against him. Her fingers sifted through his chest hair, stirring other needs inside him. "I guess our making love showed me how alone I am. How scary it is for me to be single. To be raising a child on my own.''

''After all the time we've spent together, Joy, I know you can do anything you set your mind to. You're more than capable of taking care of this baby on your own. But you don't have to. I've already offered—''

She jerked away from him. Her eyes crackled with anger. ''Was this all a part of your seduction? To get me to marry you?''

''You're the one who insisted we make love, Joy. Remember? I didn't force you into this.''

''So you just went along for the ride?''

''Don't put words into my mouth.''

''Then what? Tell me you didn't think making love to me might not convince me to marry you.''

He couldn't argue with her. He didn't want to argue with her. But how could he deny her accusation when a part of it was true? But there was more to his wanting Joy, much more. ''I thought it would bring us closer. And it did.''

''So you don't deny it.'' She sat up, raked her fingers through her tangled hair and tugged the blanket around her body.

He put a hand on her arm to keep her from fleeing. Not again. Not this time. ''I don't deny that I wanted you, that I wanted to make love to you. There's no shame in that.''

She shook her head. Her tears flowed freely, trailing down her porcelain-white cheeks. ''I believed in a fairy tale. And this is my reality.''

He took her hand and pulled her back into his embrace. Her shoulders shook with her quiet sobs.

"Reality isn't such a bad place, Joy." He kneaded her shoulders and kissed her temple. "Relax. You're a bundle of nerves. Like you said, you're hormonal. You're blowing everything out of proportion. Things will be better in the morning. You'll see."

At least he hoped so. If not, he might lose her forever.

A SHARP PAIN GRIPPED JOY and brought her awake in a split second. The sudden contraction trapped a breath in her lungs. When the invisible fist released her abdomen she gasped for air.

Slowly the fog of pain lifted from her mind. Had it been a dream? Confused, she focused on her surroundings, trying to make sense of where she was and what had jarred her so suddenly from a deep, contented sleep.

Pale sunlight slanted through the curtains along a paneled wall that she dimly recognized. The logs in the fireplace were charred but cool. A chill had swept through the room, making her want to burrow beneath the blanket that scratched her bare skin. She lay on her side, a snuggling warmth at her back. What was she doing on the floor? Reality slammed into her.

Sam. His arm was draped across her abdomen. She could feel his breath stirring the hair at her nape. Even in sleep he seemed strong and impervious to the elements.

The night's events flooded her memory and embarrassed heat suffused her skin. She couldn't think of that now. She wouldn't contemplate the consequences of once more giving him her body...and her heart.

More dire matters pressed on her. Concern quickly pushed everything else aside and panic took hold. Had she experienced a real contraction? Was she in labor? Or was it simply a nightmare?

She tried to take a few deep breaths to calm her racing heart. It was two months early for the baby. She couldn't be in labor. Or could she? Panic almost seized her but she focused on other possibilities. Taking inventory of the rest of her body, she realized she was still naked. And so was Sam.

Her joints ached. Her back hurt. Probably from sleeping on the floor all night. Which had resulted in a cramp. Not a contraction. *That's it, of course!*

Before she could sigh with relief, another contraction fisted her belly and sucked the breath right out of her. *Oh, God! This is it. This is labor. And it's too early. Way too early.*

Terrified, she struggled to sit up but she couldn't move, couldn't cry out, couldn't do anything but imagine the worst.

Sam stirred behind her. "Is it morning?" He stretched and yawned. "I should go check the cattle." His hand traced her spinal column. "And we should get dressed before—"

"Sam," she panted, "I—I...need your help." Her voice sounded calmer than her stampeding heart felt.

Immediately he pushed to a sitting position. "What's wrong?"

"I think...oh, God!...I'm in labor." A sob choked her. "Could you call the doctor?"

"Labor?" He shoved his fingers through his hair. "Are you sure?"

"No! I'm not sure about anything. But something's not right. Something's very wrong!"

"Okay, okay." He jumped to his feet but touched her head in a soothing gesture and crooned to her. "Don't worry. I'll take care of everything."

He dressed quickly, then helped Joy on with her nightshirt. "Are you comfortable here or do you want to move someplace else?"

"I'm okay."

Then another pain rocked through her. She gritted her teeth. Were contractions supposed to come this fast? She tried to remember what she'd read, what she'd been told about labor. But her mind locked onto the pain and wouldn't let go.

"Hold on to me. I'm here. I won't leave you." Sam offered his hand, which she squeezed like a vise. His eyes were dark with concern but his features remained relaxed. He covered her hand with his and caressed her knuckles with infinite tenderness. "It's okay. Try to breathe."

She couldn't. She couldn't move. She couldn't even moan. After almost a minute passed, the pain began to ease. She took a shuddering breath but continued clinging to his hand for support and strength.

"It's going away. Oh, Sam…" Tears filled her eyes. "It's too early. Is something wrong with the baby? Will we lose—"

"Shh." He knelt beside her and smoothed the wispy strands off her face. "Try to stay calm. Let's not jump to conclusions. I'm not going to let anything happen to you or to our baby.'' His gaze bore into hers. "Do you trust me?"

She nodded, her throat too tight for words to escape. She needed Sam more than she'd ever realized. She *wanted* Sam, only Sam, to be the one helping her face this.

"Okay then." His take-charge voice somehow calmed her. "I'm going to call the doctor. I'll be right back. Don't move. Don't get up. Just stay right here. If you need me, call. If another contraction starts, let me know and I'll come right back. Okay?"

Again she gave a brief nod and blinked back tears, trying to be brave, trying to slow her sprinting pulse.

While Sam made the call to the doctor, she closed her eyes and tried to breathe slowly and steadily. She rubbed her hand over her distended belly. "It's okay, little one. You're going to be okay."

Sam returned, his mouth pulled into a tight line. "Okay, here's the plan. I'm going to wake up Lacey and we're going to drop her off at your dad's. Then I'm going to drive you to the hospital. The doc will meet us there."

"And did he say anything…" She felt uncontrollable tears filling her eyes.

"He can't tell what's wrong over the phone, darlin'. He'll take a look and they'll monitor the baby and see what's happening." He reached for her hand and she grasped his with all her might, needing his strength, his solid, unwavering strength. "It's going to be all right."

She held on to Sam and prayed. *Please, God, don't let anything happen to our baby.*

SEVERAL HOURS LATER, Sam still held Joy's hand and hid his fear deep inside his heart. He didn't want to add to Joy's distress. But at the same time he faced the very real possibility that they could lose their baby.

Sam admitted to himself that the news of this baby had first been a major complication in his life. One he hadn't been too thrilled about. But now he felt the double-edged pain of guilt and regret. He wanted this baby. And Joy. He cared for them, hell, loved them so much that it brought an ache to his chest.

He felt the weight of responsibility bear down on him and remembered Joy's father's words when they'd left Lacey into his care. The older gentleman had hugged his daughter and told her everything would be all right. Then he'd clasped his hand on Sam's shoulder and walked him around the back of the truck. Out of earshot of the womenfolk, he'd said in a gruff tone, "Take care of my baby." His eyes had brimmed with tears. "She's all I have."

With a lump the size of a Colorado gold nugget in his throat, he'd driven Joy to the nearest hospital, nearly jumping out of his skin every time she experienced a contraction. He'd stayed by her side as she was settled into the labor and delivery area. From her wide-eyed expression, he knew she didn't want to be left alone. And he couldn't have imagined pacing a waiting room floor, waiting, wondering, worrying.

An IV had been inserted into Joy's arm and medicine slowly dispensed in hopes of stopping the contractions. A Velcro band had been placed around her belly to monitor the baby and the contractions. The doctor had been grim-faced and serious, the nurses efficient and kind. Their reactions only made him more petrified.

Guilt twisted its claws into his heart. This was his fault. He should never have made love to Joy last night. Damn him for his selfishness.

Joy lay on the bed, her eyes closed, her face pale as the sheet. He knew from her breathing and her strong grip on his hand that she wasn't asleep, even though the doctor had told her to rest. It had been more than three hours since her last contraction. With each passing minute, Sam had counted the seconds with tiny prayers asking for forgiveness, understanding and mercy.

The whoosh of the door opening made her eyes snap open. Sam half rose at the sight of the doctor. Neither Sam nor Joy spoke, too afraid to voice their fears, too afraid to have those fears confirmed. Instead they waited.

Doc Benton was a crusty old man with yellowing gray hair and matching mustache. His white lab coat looked too small for his oversize belly. He scuffed his feet against the linoleum when he walked, as if dragging out the inevitable news. His soft green eyes were filled with the right mixture of tenderness and candor.

"How are you feeling, young lady?" he asked, his voice like a rusty wheel.

"About the same." Joy started to sit up and the doctor pressed his hand to her shoulder. "Stay put and rest." His gaze shifted to the monitor beside the bed. "At least no contractions for a while."

Joy nodded, her eyes wide with uncertainty.

"What could have caused this to happen?" Sam asked, feeling guilt tighten its hold on him.

"It's hard to say, but probably a combination of this young lady working too hard and this baby wanting to take a peek at the world a tad early. Doctors know a lot about birthing babies, but we still can't predict when a woman's going to go into labor. And we still can't cure the common cold. Some things are just a guess. The important thing is that the contractions have stopped. And your water didn't break."

"So what do we do now?" Sam asked.

"I'd say we should probably let Joy go on home and get some much-needed rest. And I mean bed rest. Complete. I don't want you getting up for anything except to go to the bathroom. You understand?"

She nodded. "For how long?"

"Until this baby is born. I'd like to see it stay right where it is for another six to eight weeks."

"But, Doc, I can't leave Pop alone in the shop."

"You'll have to."

"What about—"

"Your job right now is to take care of yourself and this baby. No lifting. Not even your little finger. No climbing stairs. No working. No nothing.

"You can shower once a day. But that's it. And if you start to feel one contraction, you call me immediately. Understand?"

"I'll take care of it," Sam said.

"Sam—" Joy started to quarrel.

"I won't hear any arguments," Sam said, stand-

ing firm with the doctor. "You've tried to do everything by yourself for too long. Now it's my turn to
take over. I'll help your father at the shop. And I'm
going to take care of you and our baby. End of discussion."

Doc Benton gave a wry smile. "Good, then it's
all settled."

Joy remained silent until the doctor had left the
room, then she looked up at Sam. "You can't—"

"Yes, I can. You're coming home with me."

"But how—"

"The how is my problem. Not yours. You're not
going to worry about anything. I'm going to tuck
you into bed and that's where you're going to stay
until you have my baby."

"Our baby," she countered.

He grinned and bent to kiss her. "See, I told you
everything was going to be all right."

Securing Joy in his home would make it more
than all right. And it would give him an opportunity
not only to take care of her, but to make up for last
night and to show her that they could be a family.
Even out of one of her fairy tales.

Chapter Fourteen

"Don't you think I should stay at Pop's?" Joy asked as Sam parked his truck. The sun glistened off the fresh snow, making the ranch house look like Santa's cottage in the North Pole.

"Nope." Sam cut the engine, then came around to her side of the truck and lifted her into his arms, settling her firmly against his chest.

"I can walk."

"You heard the doc. No walking upstairs." He took the icy steps carefully and stamped his boots on the mat outside the front door.

"But I'm too heavy for you," she protested, even though he didn't seem the slightest winded or in a hurry to deposit her.

He grinned. "If you want to help, then open the door."

Feeling pampered and definitely lazy, she twisted the knob and pushed open the door. She felt the cold air on his leather jacket but warm as toast with his arms securely around her. "Sam, this is ridiculous. Pop can see to my needs. I should go home."

"He can't see to your needs the way I can. Now, be quiet." He entered the house.

Joy avoided looking toward the fireplace where they'd made love last night. In retrospect it seemed a foolish thing to do. Still, she felt as if making love and surviving the scare at the hospital had forged an even deeper bond between them.

Sam climbed the stairs carefully and carried her right past the guest room.

Her nerves tangled into fine knots. "Where are we going?"

"To my bed."

"Sam!"

"Quit arguing with me. I'm not going to seduce you."

She wasn't sure if that brought relief or disappointment. "I didn't think you were. But…"

"This is the most comfortable bed in the house and it's the closest to a bathroom so you won't have far to walk."

"I wouldn't have to walk at all if you had your way."

He grinned and gave her a flirtatious wink. "Now you're catching on."

"Are you sure this is…well, proper? I mean, we're not married."

"I can take care of that with a phone call."

Part of her was tempted, but she resisted. She wouldn't marry Sam without knowing that he loved her and wanted her, not just their baby. "Not today."

"Too tired to consider a honeymoon?" His eyes gleamed with humor.

She slapped his shoulder playfully and settled her arm more securely around his neck. A new doubt troubled her. "Where are you going to sleep?"

"Close by." He eased open the door to his bedroom, nudging it with his broad shoulder. "In case you need me in the night."

Practical. Everything he'd said was practical. She couldn't argue with his logic, but the reasons brought a sharp ache to her chest. He didn't love her. As absurd as it seemed, after the long day they'd shared at the hospital, she wanted romance, passion, expressions of love. But she knew that was more than Sam had to offer. Bitter tears burned the backs of her eyes.

She tried to ignore the constant pain jabbing her heart like a blunt knife and focused on Sam's room. She shouldn't have been surprised that everything was neat and tidy, exactly like Sam. A simple but beautiful quilt in bold colors of blue, burgundy and green covered the mattress. An overstuffed chair occupied much of one corner, and a stately armoire stood guard against one wall. On the bedside table, only a clock radio took up space. Covering the hardwood floor was a faded Native American rug. Where once the colors looked to have been vibrant yellow and red, they were toned down to maize, with the warmth of the setting sun.

Sam placed Joy in the chair next to the bed. His hands slid easily away from her and left her chilled without his warmth and nearness. "Rest here while I change the sheets."

"Sam—"

He ignored her protest and went about unmaking

the bed, then remaking it. He moved quickly and efficiently, as if used to household chores. When he folded back the covers, he returned to Joy's side and helped into bed, removing her shoes and pulling the quilt up to her chin. It was a sweet gesture without any sexual overtones. Which only frustrated Joy more.

Not that she wanted him to make a pass at her. Heck, they couldn't have made love if they'd wanted to! The doctor had said so. But why didn't Sam want to? She needed more than reassurance. She needed him to tell her he loved her.

"I'll set out some towels in the bathroom. What else do you need?"

You, here in bed with me. For you to whisper in my ear that everything is going to be all right. For you to hold me close. For you to tell me that you love me. "Nothing. I'm fine, Sam."

"Do you need anything to drink? Are you hungry?"

"No, thanks."

"You're probably tired. Try to get some sleep."

She nodded and tried to reassure herself that he was being considerate, not cold and distant. Her heart twisted with uncertainty. But was he being considerate for her...or just for the baby?

THE FIRST DAY PASSED more quickly than Joy anticipated. Bewildered, amused then concerned, she watched Sam come and go. He always seemed to be nearby, hovering, worrying, fussing. The awkwardness between them eased and she realized he was simply being a good nurse. Not too intrusive. But always eager to help. Still, she wished for his touch, his arms to hold her, for those words he couldn't seem to say.

Late that night, he brought her hot chocolate and a bowl of her favorite craving—hazelnut ice cream and pickles.

"Oh, Sam! Have you been hiding this downstairs?"

"I stopped at the grocery store when I picked up Lacey from your father's." He frowned as she scooped a large helping into her mouth. "Looks disgusting."

"The baby wants it," she argued. She licked the spoon and leaned back against the headboard, sighing with contentment at the creamy rich texture melting across her tongue.

"Then you can have all you want."

"I'll share," she said, offering him a taste.

"No, thanks." He settled into the chair beside the bed, leaned back and stretched out his long legs.

"You're not going to sleep there, are you?"

He shook his head. "Nope."

Her heart started to pound with hope. Maybe... maybe he'd crawl into bed with her and hold her through the night, calm her fears, make her feel more like a woman than a patient. "Then where?"

"Down the hall." He gripped the arms of the chair. "If you're tired, then I'll say good-night."

"No, no, that's okay. I'd like some company. It's been awfully quiet today."

"I'll bring the television upstairs tomorrow morning and set it up."

"That's not the company I was hoping for."

He rubbed his jaw, then his gaze snagged hers. "Oh, well…good." A grin spread slowly across his face. "How are you feeling?"

"You already asked me that tonight, Sam."

"I wanted to make sure nothing had changed."

"It hasn't. How are you?"

He stared at her for a minute before answering. "Okay."

"I bet you're tired after all the running around you did today."

He shrugged. "I'm not the one carrying a baby."

She gave a slight nod but felt disappointment well inside her. Couldn't they talk about anything but the baby? "Where's Lacey?"

"In bed. Sleeping, I hope."

"Was she easier to put down tonight?"

"Yeah. She was worried about you, though." His gaze locked onto hers. "Me, too."

Her heart skipped a beat. "I told you I'm okay."

"You certainly gave me a scare today." He plowed his fingers through his hair. "I don't know what I'd do if something happened to—" He stopped before finishing his thought.

Her heart pounded. Had he been worried about her or just the baby? She swallowed the need to ask him but couldn't stifle a yawn.

"You're tired," he said, standing. He took the empty bowl from her and pressed a chaste kiss to her cheek. "G'night. I'll be right down the hall if you need me."

LATE IN THE NIGHT, she stirred from a vivid dream of Sam kissing her neck and massaging her back.

She blinked against the darkness and shifted beneath the quilt. Her skin prickled with heat. A heat aroused by the memory of Sam's kisses. Then she saw him.

He stood in the doorway, a pale light from down the hall silhouetting his rock-solid frame. He watched her silently.

"Are you still up?" she asked.

"Just checking on you." His voice sounded deep and full as if it could surround her like his solid embrace. "Go back to sleep."

His presence gave her a sense of peace. Sliding back beneath the covers, she fell asleep, knowing he was nearby watching over her, protecting her and their baby.

THE NEXT FEW MORNINGS they settled into a routine. The moment she sat up in bed, Sam stepped into the room, as if he'd been waiting and watching for her to awaken.

"How'd you sleep?" he asked, bringing her a cup of tea.

"Like a baby."

"No more contractions?"

"Not a one."

"Are you warm enough?"

"Yes."

"Hungry?"

"You have to ask?" She smiled.

He stuck his hands in his back pockets. His flannel shirt stretched across his chest and shoulders, reminding her of his solid strength and powerful muscles. "How about pancakes this morning?"

"Don't go to any trouble. Toast or cereal is okay."

"You need something to stick to your ribs."

"Believe me, there's enough sticking to my ribs these days."

He grinned, erasing his serious expression. "Has the baby been moving?"

"Constantly."

"Good." He gave a brief nod. "Okay, I'll be back in a few minutes with breakfast."

LACEY MADE IT A HABIT of eating upstairs with Joy while Sam handled his chores at the barn. Joy appreciated the company, for she knew the rest of the day would be quiet and uneventful. Or at least she hoped so.

"Daddy's gonna take me horseback ridin' this afternoon," Lacey said one morning after Joy had been there a week.

"That will be fun. You like to ride, don't you?"

"Uh-huh. Daddy sits me in front of him. When I'm bigger I'm gonna have my own horse."

Joy smiled and nibbled on her toast.

"When can you make me those pancakes you promised?"

"How about after the baby comes?" Joy answered.

"Okay." The little girl's brow furrowed and pinched her eyebrows together. "Daddy said you gotta stay in bed till then."

"That's right."

"Is the baby okay?" She poked her finger at Joy's tummy.

Joy covered the little girl's curious hand, flattening it against the roundness of her stomach. "Yes. We just want to make sure it stays there until it's time for it to come out."

The little girl nodded like a wise old woman. "Where are we gonna put the baby?"

"I don't know," she answered, her chest tightening with raw emotions. There were so many unanswered questions, so many things that needed to be done. But she couldn't think of them now; she couldn't do anything stuck in this bed. She had to block out the need to ready a nursery and buy diapers and baby clothes. She had to concentrate on keeping the baby safe.

"Daddy says this is gonna be my little sister."

"That's right. Do you want a little sister?"

"Yeah! You know what?"

"What?"

Lacey's eyes grew round. "Oops!" She clamped her hand over her mouth. "I'm not supposed to tell."

"A secret, huh?"

The little girl nodded.

"Well, Christmas is a time for secrets."

Lacey grinned. "Christmas presents. Do you know what Santa's gonna get me?"

"No, what?"

She gave a noncommittal shrug. "I dunno. I don't think he can get it."

"Well, you never know about Santa. He's a pretty smart fellow."

Lacey's tone and demeanor had turned too serious for a five-year-old. She munched a piece of toast thoughtfully. "What are you gonna name the baby?"

"Do you have any suggestions?" Maybe tonight she'd discuss possible names with Sam.

"I like Shelley."

"That's a pretty name. We'll ask your daddy about it later."

After finishing most of her egg and sausage, Lacey slanted her gaze toward Joy. "Are you gonna be my mama?"

The little girl's question ripped the breath out of Joy's lungs. "Well, um, Lacey…" What should she say? What could she say? "Don't you already have a mama?"

Lacey shrugged. "I guess." She drew the tines of her fork through the egg and smeared yolk across her plate. "But she don't really want me no more."

"Oh, Lacey!" Joy patted the bed beside her and the little girl climbed up and snuggled close. Her chest aching for the little girl, she smoothed her hand over her hair. "Why do you say that?"

"'Cause it's true. She wanted to get rid of me. Said I was a noonsense."

A nuisance? What mother would tell her child that? A sorry mother. A mother who didn't love her child. Tears welled in Joy's eyes. She hugged Lacey and pressed a kiss to her forehead. "Don't worry, sweetheart. You can say I'm your mama if you want."

Tilting her face toward Joy, Lacey gave her a watery smile. "Does that mean you and Daddy are gonna get married?"

Joy couldn't miss the enthusiasm in the little girl's

voice or the need in her eyes. She pushed back the urge to agree. How could she? How could she marry a man who didn't love her? But did she really have a choice anymore?

Resting her cheek against the little girl's head, Joy whispered, "I don't know. I really don't know."

AFTER JOY HAD BEEN at the ranch one week, Sam had established a careful routine, which not only gave her a sense of security but also exaggerated her boredom. After breakfast and chores at the barn, he drove Lacey to school. Armed with a beeper and cellular phone, he then went to the shop, where he helped her father unload boxes and take care of customers. Joy was given strict instructions to call if she needed anything. Just to be sure, he called to check on her every hour. His thoughtfulness touched her and drove her crazy at the same time.

By noon each day, he brought her lunch, but she rarely saw him eat. After seeing to her needs and household chores, he raced to pick Lacey up from school and together they helped in the store the rest of the afternoon. Joy felt exhausted just watching him go from one chore to the next, ending the day back at the barn tending to the horses and cattle.

When she thought he'd be ready to call it a night, he'd read Lacey a story, put her to bed and then sit beside Joy to keep her company. He brought her books and magazines that he thought might interest her. But nothing, no bestseller, television show or movie could capture her attention the way he did. His thoughtfulness moved her, his concern endeared her to him, but she ached with the burning question that never seemed to be answered. Did he love her? Could he love her?

"We're home," he said, breaking the silence and her morose mood with his easy smile.

"So Lacey's out of school for the holidays?"

"Yep." He remained in the hallway, partially hidden by the door. "She's unloading her stuff. More cookies and candies from the school party. I'm sure she'll be right up. Can I get you anything?"

"No, I'm fine."

"You're feeling okay?"

"Yes." Her hands twisted the sheet with exasperation. She knew he wasn't asking about her but about the baby. "But I wanted to talk to you about something."

His brow furrowed and he moved closer, but he still remained in the hallway. "What's wrong?"

"Nothing really. I wanted to see if you'd bought Lacey's Christmas present."

"Uh…" His gaze darted to the side. "Can we discuss that later?"

"Sure." Strange, she thought, he usually jumped at the chance to discuss Lacey's Christmas.

"Anything else?"

"Well, we haven't discussed a name yet." She smoothed a hand over her stomach. She'd never really included Sam in any of the baby preparations. But she figured it was time.

He seemed to sense the magnitude of her statement and leaned a shoulder against the door facing. "I guess I thought you'd name the baby after your mother."

She lifted her gaze and tears burned the backs of her eyes. "That's okay with you?"

"Sure. Of course, you haven't told me her name yet. It's not Fred, is it?"

She laughed, sniffing back the tears. "Christine."

He repeated the name, rolling it over his tongue, testing it. "I like it. I like it a lot."

Relieved, she leaned back into the pillows and smiled.

"Would you like a little company this afternoon?" he asked.

She touched her hand to her hair. "Come on in and sit a spell."

He grinned. "I didn't mean me. You've got company."

"But I wasn't expecting anyone. I must look—"

"Beautiful."

She folded the covers back over her rounded belly. "Who's here?"

Sam grinned and stepped inside the room. He carried a bunch of pink balloons that reached almost to the ceiling. "A few friends."

"Happy baby!" someone shouted from behind him.

Then a stream of friends and neighbors flowed into her room, each carrying a package. They filed around the bed, putting the presents at the footboard.

Smiling from ear to ear, Lacey bounded onto the bed beside her. "Are you surprised?"

Stunned, Joy touched her face, wondering if this was some kind of a dream.

Pop entered and dropped a kiss on her forehead. "How are you, sugar?"

"Fine, Pop. How's the shop?"

"Locked up tight for the evening. Couldn't miss this baby shower."

She blinked back tears. "But who...how...?"

"Sam did everything," Edna Warren said, handing out paper plates decorated with bottles and bears and diapered babies.

Joy stared at Sam with disbelief. "You did this?"

"Guilty as charged. But I had a lot of help."

"But—"

He cupped her face and smiled. "No buts. Just enjoy yourself. But don't overdo it. Okay?"

Charlie Foster passed around a tray of tiny sandwiches and Pop cut a cake that had been decorated to resemble a stork carrying a bundled package.

"When can we open the presents?" Lacey asked.

Everyone laughed.

"Right now seems like a good time." Pop handed Joy the first package.

"You all shouldn't have done this."

"Every new mother should have a baby shower," Mrs. Warren stated. "We're all simply delighted you're gonna have this baby. But not too soon. You hear?"

Joy gave them a watery smile, then began opening the present her father had given her. Inside was a frilly pink infant's gown. "Oh, Pop! It's beautiful."

He sniffed roughly. "Thought my grandbaby needed something to wear home from the hospital."

"Thanks, Earl," Sam said. "I just hope the doc is right and that this is a girl. I'd hate to have my son wearing something like that."

"Wouldn't matter at that age, anyway," Pop said with a grin.

One after another, Joy opened the presents, her gaze automatically shifting to Sam to show him what they'd received. Strange how it felt as if they were a regular married couple with him standing nearby, offering to help with ribbons or cutting tape on boxes. He seemed interested in everything, from the big box of diapers to the little hairbrush and fingernail clippers.

"Thank you everyone for everything," Joy said, feeling her throat constrict once again. "You were too generous."

"That's not all," Sam said, stepping out of the room. When he returned, he rolled in a white eyelet-covered bassinet. Joy couldn't stop the rush of tears as she imagined her baby sleeping peacefully in the downy cloud.

"Oh, Sam! It's beautiful."

"Only the best for my daughters." He kissed Lacey, then touched Joy's stomach protectively, possessively. Her heart swelled.

"But that's not all, Daddy!" Lacey bounced on the bed. "Can we show her now? Can we?"

Sam smiled and nodded.

"You gotta come see, Joy." Lacey grabbed her hand and tugged.

"Is this the secret you've been holding inside you for so long?" Joy asked.

Lacey nodded and jumped off the bed.

Eager to see the big surprise, Joy shoved aside the covers, but Sam stopped her with a disapproving frown. "Not so fast, darlin'."

He bent and scooped her up into his arms. Carrying her down the hallway, he entered the guest room, where she'd once stayed and where she'd thought Sam was sleeping each night. But the room had been transformed into a fairy-tale nursery.

The walls had been freshly painted a soft yellow. A white crib took precedence in the room and was adorned with a flowery sunflower comforter. Matching drapes and a wallpaper border made it complete.

"I can't believe you did this." Her voice shook with raw emotion.

"Do you like it?" His voice sounded thick, uncertain.

She should be angry at his audacity. She should be furious at his presumption that she would give in and marry him, that their child would live here. But she wasn't. Her feelings were a hundred and eighty degrees in the opposite direction. His generosity and sweetness touched her more than she could have ever anticipated.

"I love it." She met his gaze, saw the depth of emotion churning in his eyes, then hugged him close. His arms tightened around her, made her feel secure and cared for. Was that enough? Could she live with that? So many women wished they had this much care and concern from their husbands. So many relationships lacked even this much tender affection. Or would she always feel the relationship was half empty instead of half full?

Feeling the guests crowd in behind them, she pushed aside her questions for the time being. "How did you know that's the bedding I wanted?"

"Santa's little elves don't keep secrets very well."

If only Sam would love her this much. But maybe his love for their child was enough. Maybe she could live with that after all.

"So," Charlie Foster said, giving the nursery a nodding approval, "when are you two going to make this union official?"

Sam gave Joy a gentle squeeze. "Whenever the lady gives me the okay."

But she was waiting to hear those three little words from him. Would she be waiting forever?

Chapter Fifteen

"I'll have a b-b-blue Christmas without you." Elvis Presley's voice warbled through the house.

Sam smiled, imagining his daughter singing her heart out downstairs as once more she repositioned the wrapped packages under the tree. He'd finally agreed she could open one present tonight on Christmas Eve. But he'd choose the gift—a cuddly stuffed animal he'd found at Joy's shop. Tomorrow she'd get her real gift.

Turning his concentration back to Joy's present, he wadded up the wrapping paper, tossed it with the other crumpled attempts in the trash and started over. The black velvet box was too small and irregular. But he wanted it to look perfect. Again he cut the gold foil paper that matched the solid gold band and diamond engagement ring inside, folded it over the box and taped the underside. Once more he tried to make the ends look neat as he creased and taped them.

"Damn." He was beginning to think he should give Joy the box unwrapped.

The ribbon he stuck on the top overpowered the

tiny box and made the whole thing look ridiculous. Frowning, he reached for the roll of wrapping paper again. If Joy didn't say yes this time, he knew he'd have the bluest Christmas on record. And it wouldn't have anything to do with the freezing weather outside.

"Daddy!" Lacey's voice carried over the twang of the steel guitar.

"What, darlin'?"

"Can I open my present now?"

He grinned and shook his head. It was going to be a long afternoon. And a longer night, if Joy said no when he gave her this gift at midnight.

"HAVE YOU WRAPPED Lacey's presents?" Joy asked, after Sam had put his daughter to bed. She had no doubt he'd been as thorough with his daughter's Christmas gifts as he had been with her baby shower.

"I wrapped some. But they wouldn't win any contests. Would you like to go sit beside the tree, watch the lights, see if Lacey tore any paper as she was reorganizing the presents again tonight?"

Joy smiled and stretched. "I think I'd like to wait till the morning. I'm kind of tired and…well, there's always something so magical about seeing a tree on Christmas morning."

He gave a nod and grew silent. She wondered if he was stewing over his package-wrapping technique. He'd seemed uncertain and jittery all evening.

"You know, Sam, there aren't any contests for wrapping packages that I know of. Lacey doesn't care what the outside looks like. She's more interested in the inside.''

"You're probably right. But I want it to be perfect.''

"It will be.''

He sighed and leaned back in the chair he occupied most evenings in what was now her room. "I don't know what to do with Santa's gifts. Should I wrap them? Leave them unwrapped? Set them up? Leave them in their boxes? What?''

"What did Santa do at your house when you were little?'' she asked, knowing there were as many answers to his question as there were households celebrating Christmas in the world.

"Santa never came to my house.'' His voice was matter-of-fact, but she read the tightness around his mouth as deeply etched pain.

Her heart contracted. Her eyes immediately filled with tears for the little boy who'd had no Christmas. No wonder he wanted this Christmas to be special for Lacey. For him, too.

"Never?'' she asked, stunned by his response. She remembered what he'd told her about his parents, but she'd always thought he'd enjoyed a few Christmases as a small boy. With her own background, it was almost impossible to imagine a child never experiencing a real Christmas. Could that be another reason why he found it so difficult to open his heart and love?

"I told you about that silver tree. But my mother left right before Christmas. I guess that's when I learned Santa didn't exist.''

"Oh, Sam—''

"It's no big deal." He crossed his arms over his chest in an effort to block her sympathy. "My ex-wife used to put Santa's gifts to Lacey unwrapped around the tree. I didn't know if that was how it was supposed to be done or not."

"It can be done any way you choose. Lacey will be the most excited little girl come morning. She'll rip into her presents so fast that it won't matter if you wrapped them or not." Smiling softly, Joy added, "She loved the cute seal you gave her tonight."

"I found it in your shop. I remembered her playing with all those stuffed toys a few weeks ago when we were looking for lights, when I discovered or learned that you were..." The tension eased from his strained features as his focus settled on Joy's rounded belly. "How's the baby tonight? Restless?"

"I think sleeping right now."

"Amazing to think of a whole little human being tucked inside you." His eyes grew moist and emotions enveloped her. Sam linked his fingers together and pushed his hands outward to stretch and pop his knuckles, breaking the poignant moment. "Lacey had to sleep with it...the seal. So it must have been a success."

"Of course it was."

"I guess we're ready then for tomorrow." He started to rise.

"Good. Pop's going to be out early in the morning. He picked up a couple of gifts for Lacey from me."

"You didn't have to do that."

She smiled. "I didn't...couldn't. But I wanted

to." She rubbed the base of her back where a dull pain had been bothering her most of the day. She'd probably been lying in bed too much. Of course, these days it seemed strange when something didn't ache. "Did you remember to get something for her stocking?"

"Sure did. And yours, too."

"Oh, Sam. You didn't have to do that. You gave me so much the other day at the shower." Again she felt a tightness in her chest and blinked away sentimental tears. "What about Lacey's big gift? What did you figure out that she wanted?"

"You were right. Santa wouldn't divulge any secrets. But I think she'll like what I got for her."

Joy smiled, knowing Lacey already had what she wanted—an attentive, loving father. "Do you need help wrapping it?"

"Nope. It can't be wrapped."

Surprised by his answer, she felt a bubble of laughter rise in her throat. "What did you get? A car?"

"A horse. A pony, actually." His brow furrowed with concern. "Think she'll like that?"

"She's already the luckiest little girl in the world. And I think she'll be ecstatic. She's always talking about when you take her riding on your horse. So I'm sure she'll love having her own so she can ride alongside you."

He released a held breath. "I just hope it's what she truly wants."

"It will be." Shifting beneath the covers, she felt more and more confined to this bed, as if she wore chains hooked to the bedposts.

"Uncomfortable?"

"Sam, at this stage in my pregnancy, there is no such thing as comfortable."

"Is your back still hurting?"

"A little."

"Want me to massage it?"

Her skin tingled with awareness as she remembered the massage he'd given her a week ago, which had led to their making love. No chance of that happening tonight. But his gentle kneading might alleviate some of the tension along her spine. "Okay. Question is, how do we do this?"

"Whatever is com—" He grinned. "Get in any position you want. You can sit up and lean forward or lie on your side."

She nodded, well aware that her body seemed to no longer belong to her anymore. Rolling to her side, she tucked a pillow beneath her belly. Then she froze with shock. "Oh, my!"

"What?" Sam asked, immediately on his feet.

She stared up at him, reading the concern in his dark eyes. Her heart jolted into overdrive. Her hands started trembling with dread and fear. Automatically she reached for him. "I think my water just broke."

Sam squeezed her hand. "I'll call the doc."

DOC BENTON TOUCHED her shoulder. His eyes were calm and sincere, and Joy locked onto his gaze as if it were a lifeline.

"Looks like you're going to get a Christmas baby." He gave her a tender smile.

"The labor can't be stopped?" Sam asked, stand-

ing on the other side of the hospital bed, still holding
Joy's hand.

"Not once her water is broken. Then you have
about twenty-four hours to deliver before you have
to worry about infection that could set in and harm
the baby and the mother." Doc Benton, who'd been
her family physician since she was a baby, patted
her shoulder, then reached for her chart to scribble
some notes. "It will be a few hours, I'd say. You're
dilated to three."

The doc's penetrating gaze shifted to Sam. "Is he
gonna stay with you, Joy?"

"I'm staying," Sam stated.

"It's not up to you," the doc said. "How do you
feel, Joy? Would you be more comfortable with him
in the waiting room?"

She looked up at Sam and knew she wanted this
man beside her for the rest of her life. She needed
him, wanted to share this moment with him. "No,
I'd like Sam to stay."

"Very well." The doc headed for the door. "A
nurse will be in to check on you periodically. If you
need anything, push the nurse's button. I'm going
to call in a neonatologist."

Joy's body went rigid with fear. "Wh-why?"

"We already know this baby is a preemie. Better
safe than sorry. We don't want to take any
chances."

Sam squeezed her hand for support. "Whatever
you think is best, Doc."

THE MINUTES MOVED in slow motion, making the
hours seem more like days. Sam wiped Joy's brow

with a washcloth and fed her ice chips, keeping an eye on the monitor. "Here comes another contraction," he said. He could almost feel the pain rip through his own body as he watched her face contort. "Hang on to me."

Finally, when Sam thought she couldn't stand any more assaults on her exhausted body, the doctor announced it was time to push. From that moment on, a whirlwind of activity swirled around them. It seemed like the old days when he was saddled to a bucking bronc, spinning round and round, catching only glimpses and flashes in a vortex of color and noise as his ears roared and his heart pummeled his chest.

Joy gripped his hand as he'd once clung to a saddle horn. It felt as if they were the only two in the maelstrom of activity. Somehow they'd ride this out together.

His breathing felt as labored as Joy's. He counted through each contraction, telling her when to push and when to stop. It was both exhilarating, knowing he was an integral part of bringing his baby into the world, and petrifying.

"There's the head," Doc Benton announced. "See it?"

Feeling a lump form in his throat, Sam could only nod.

"Won't be long now. The next push should do it, Joy."

"Here's another contraction," the nurse said.

Automatically Sam started with "One, two, three…"

As he counted by rote memory, an irrational thought occurred to him. What if the baby couldn't breathe? Why didn't they hurry? His child could suffocate!

"Shouldn't you hurry?" He felt a ball of panic wedge in his gut. "What are you waiting for?"

Doc Benton ignored him. The nurse held a blue sheet to wrap the baby in. Then his baby emerged all wrinkly and wet and crying a high-pitched wail. Joy sighed and laughed at the same time. She looked toward Sam, her eyes full of joyful tears. He wanted to tell her so much—how grateful he was to her, how full his life was, how complete she'd made it, how he loved her. But he couldn't get the words out.

"It's a boy!" Doc Benton said, handling the baby deftly.

"A boy?" Sam echoed, looking closer.

"Never been wrong about a thing like that." The doc clipped the umbilical cord and gave the baby to the nurse.

Sam's gaze collided with Joy's startled one. "But you said..."

"It's a boy?" she asked. Then she started laughing. "Well, it'll be the prettiest boy in town with all those frilly pink clothes."

Then the room fell into an awkward silence. The baby was no longer crying. As if sensing something was wrong, Joy reached for Sam's hand. And the nurse rushed out of the labor and delivery room with the baby in a hospital bassinet.

SAM SAT BESIDE HER BED, his features ragged with raw emotion, his body like a stone, stiff and unresponsive.

Joy felt her world caving in on her. Tears streamed down her cheeks, dampening her hospital gown.

Nurses came and went quietly, taking her temperature and blood pressure and trying to offer comfort. But no one had words to mend the fracture in her heart. No one could alleviate the guilt she felt. No one could erase the grief.

It sounded like a funeral parlor in the hospital room. She tried not to think of it that way. But fear lodged in her chest. What if their son died?

Their son. They'd had a beautiful son who weighed a few ounces over three pounds. So tiny. So vulnerable. So precious.

Right now he was in the nursery ICU struggling for each breath, for his very life. The neonatologist had suggested that they return to her designated room. He'd keep them posted on their baby's progress.

Would it be good news? Or bad?

And what would that mean? She'd started to believe that Sam and she could form a family with Lacey and their son. But without a child to bring into the circle, she would be an outcast. Unwanted. Unloved. Alone.

Her heart shattered into tiny shards.

SAM WAS STUNNED. He felt numb from the inside out. He couldn't move or think.

A part of him would shrivel and die if his son

didn't survive. But it was more than the fear of losing their tiny baby. Much more.

His gaze settled on Joy. He'd lose her, too. If their child died, she would have no reason to marry him. And he desperately needed her to be with him. Forever. He understood now his reason wasn't simply to form a family or because Joy would make an excellent mother to Lacey. It was a purely selfish reason. He loved her.

He couldn't lose her, too. If the neonatologist would allow him to help out in the nursery ICU, then he'd fight desperately for his baby's life. But since he was stuck here, waiting, wondering, praying, he'd fight for the one thing he could try to save.

Pushing himself up from the chair beside her bed, he went to Joy. He handed her his handkerchief. "It's going to be okay."

She turned a tear-ravaged face toward him. "What if it's not? What if he doesn't…"

"Don't say it. We have to think positive. If not for us, for that tiny little baby down the hall. We're all he's got. We're not going to lose him."

"It's my fault," she said, her voice hoarse.

"No, it's not." He cupped her face. "Joy, look at me. You did everything you could to keep from going into labor. Sometimes things happen. We don't always see the reason. Just like there was a reason we met in Denver. A reason you came into my life when you did. A reason you became pregnant. I couldn't see the reasons then. But I can now."

"Sam—"

"Let me finish." He knelt beside her bed and held

her hands. "You've changed me, Joy. Made me a better man. A better father. And I hope a better husband."

"What are you saying?"

"That I want to marry you, Joy. Not because it's the right thing to do. Not because our son needs a family. All that is true. But the only reason I care about at this moment is…" His throat tightened. He looked deep into her blue eyes and found the courage to admit his weakness. Something he'd always fought against. "I love you."

"Oh, Sam…"

"Will you marry me, Joy? No matter what happens today or tomorrow or next week or next year. Will you stand by me? Face the future with me? Will you be my wife?"

Dipping her hands, she began to weep. Her shoulders shook. Warm, wet tears splashed on their joined hands. His heart stilled. Maybe she didn't love him. Maybe she wished she'd never met him. Maybe he'd waited too long to tell her his feelings. Maybe it was just too damn late.

Whatever she felt, he had to know the truth. "Joy?"

She met his gaze. Slowly, beatifically, her face transformed, her mouth lifting in a hesitant smile. "I've waited forever for you to say those words. Do you mean them?"

"With all my heart and soul." He kissed her forehead and pulled her against his chest. "Could you…someday…learn to love me?"

Her arms tightened around his neck. "I already do, Sam. I already do."

"Then you'll marry me?"

"Yes. Oh, yes."

Sam held her, cherishing every second. She clung to him. Somehow the dark, fearful night facing them didn't seem as scary with their love shining from within.

"SANTA WAS A LITTLE LATE this year." Lacey stood amid an avalanche of wrapping paper.

"But it was well worth the wait," Joy said. The tree lights glinted off the sparkling diamond ring on her left hand. Her heart swelled with hope and promise.

"We're probably the only family in Jingle that still has their Christmas tree up." Sam sat beside her, his fingers linked with hers.

"Do you mind?" Earl asked from his position beside the tree.

"Not at all. I don't care if we keep it up year-round. Christmas has become my favorite holiday."

"It's definitely a day of miracles." Joy gave his hand a gentle squeeze.

A tiny cry punctured the air. Each family member paused and looked toward the stairwell.

"I'll go get little Christopher." Her little Kris Kringle. Her mother must have been watching over him like a guardian angel, protecting him during those scary first few days. The baby had turned the corner and begun to thrive. He'd only had to stay in the hospital two weeks before they brought him home. Where he belonged.

"Let me." Sam gave her leg a pat.

A moment later he came down the stairs holding

the small bundle in his arms. A tiny arm pushed out of the blanket. "I think he wants his mama." He gave Joy a smile that filled her with longing. "Me, too, son. Me, too."

Cuddling their baby boy between them, Joy looked into Sam's flannel-gray eyes and knew she'd found the life she'd longed for—a home, a family, a man with a heart big enough to love her for all eternity.

"There really is a Santa!" Lacey exclaimed.

"How do you know?" Pop asked, hooking his arm around his new granddaughter's shoulders.

"'Cuz he brought me what I wanted. A real family!"

Look for Leanna Wilson's next book,
THE THIRD KISS, a Silhouette Romance,
in November 2000.

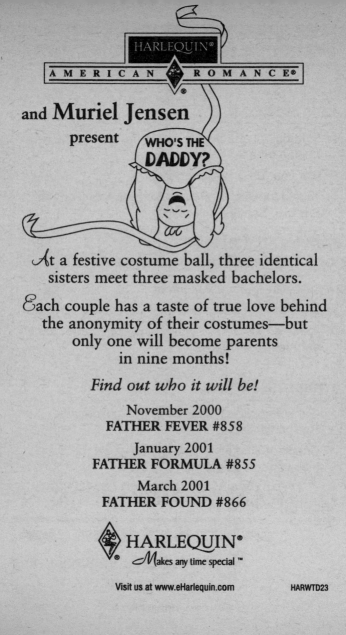

HARLEQUIN

A M E R I C A N ◆ **R O M A N C E**

and **Muriel Jensen**
present

WHO'S THE DADDY?

*A*t a festive costume ball, three identical
sisters meet three masked bachelors.

*E*ach couple has a taste of true love behind
the anonymity of their costumes—but
only one will become parents
in nine months!

Find out who it will be!

November 2000
FATHER FEVER #858

January 2001
FATHER FORMULA #855

March 2001
FATHER FOUND #866

HARLEQUIN®
Makes any time special ™

COMING NEXT MONTH

#849 SECRET BABY SPENCER by Jule McBride
Return to Tyler
Businessman Seth Spencer was surprised to see Jenna Robinson in Tyler,
Wisconsin, especially once he discovered she was pregnant—with his
baby! Though she claimed she planned to marry another, Seth was not
about to let Jenna's secret baby carry any other name but Spencer.

#850 FATHER FEVER by Muriel Jensen
Who's the Daddy?
Was he the father of Athena Ames's baby? Was the enigmatic beauty even
really expecting? Carefree bachelor David Hartford was determined to
uncover the truth and see if Athena was behind his sudden case of father
fever!

#851 CATCHING HIS EYE by Jo Leigh
The Girlfriends' Guide to...
Plain Jane Emily Proctor knew her chance had come to catch the eye of
her lifelong crush. With a little help from friends—and one great big
makeover—could Emily finally win her heart's desire?

#852 THE MARRIAGE PORTRAIT by Pamela Bauer
Happily Wedded After
When Cassandra Carrigan accepted Michael McFerrin's marriage of
convenience proposal, she'd thought it was a sound business deal. But
spending night after night with her "husband" soon had her hoping
Michael would consider mixing a little business with a lot of pleasure....

Visit us at www.eHarlequin.com